Complete Creation by Andy Riedlinger

Edited by Patty Schaff

Original Black & White Edition 2024

www.identityofoliver.com

Andy Riedlinger
About the Author

Andy Riedlinger was born and raised in Williston, North Dakota, and has many fond memories of growing up in his hometown. He still has several good friends living in western North Dakota and often returns to see them. This rural atmosphere provided plenty of inspiration for Hometown Chronicles, the first novel in the Identity of Oliver Series.

Andy has wonderful parents, whose mother worked as a schoolteacher and whose father worked as a manager in a bustling oil patch called the Bakken. After raising their family, they moved to a retirement community in Ft Myers, Florida, which they absolutely love. He also has two younger sisters, who are each enjoying great careers and family life. One of his younger sisters, who now lives in Tennessee, has four wonderful children and a loving husband who has blessed their family with a thriving chiropractic business. His youngest sister became a pharmaceutical doctor and is raising one delightful child with her charismatic husband, with whom Andy enjoys fishing with when visiting North Dakota.

Andy moved to Fort Collins, Colorado, immediately after graduating high school in 1997 to pursue new adventures and his love for the mountains. In 2001, he graduated from college with a degree in video production and has since become a respected video systems engineer for many of the largest productions in Colorado. He is also a successful entrepreneur who has pursued many business interests in the city of Denver, where he currently lives. He has owned businesses in Colorado's marijuana industry, real estate market, audiovisual industry, as well as two laundromats and a small vending business.

Andy enjoys fishing, hunting, snowboarding, snowmobiling, billiards, oil painting, writing, and traveling in his free time. He began writing at a young age and has continued to chase his dream of being a successful author. Remarkably, he had written some short stories, several poems, and a novella before he even graduated high school. He published his first novel in 2007 and has written a number of unique pieces of literature, including five novels, two novellas, short stories, an autobiography, and over one hundred poems.

The Identity of Oliver Series

Author

Andy Riedlinger

The Identity of Oliver Series

Hometown Chronicles is the first book in The Identity of Oliver Series. This remarkable story will introduce you to a handful of exciting characters and their unique relationship with Oliver. Each one of these characters has its own tantalizing story to tell and unique influence over the anomalies Oliver faces. This book explains an incredible love interest and friendships whose futures hang in the balance of small-town injustice. Hometown Chronicles is a philosophical think piece with an intense narrative of true love, unique integrity, and a goal for revenge served ice cold. Be prepared to experience a whirlwind of emotions as this amazing tale of bizarre fate is told. This story will be sure to make you laugh and cry as you read what causes Oliver to embark on extraordinary journeys around the world.

West Coast Chronicles is the second book in The Identity of Oliver Series. This story follows the twisted fate of a young man fleeing from corrupt law enforcement. Oliver takes you up and down America's West Coast on an exuberant adventure in search of his evil nemesis and hippy friend to help save the life of the father to his love interest. However, this isn't a story that only explains physical exploration. It will also lead you on a quest to understand some of life's most intriguing questions and difficult problems to solve. The unique subplots of this book are guaranteed to leave you rolling on the floor with laughter, wiping away tears of sadness, and pondering over the many complex issues Oliver faces. Interactions with punk rockers, ravers, and hippies explain their unique subculture dancing in the lives of ordinary people. West Coast Chronicles will leave you with an intense cliffhanger with its philosophies standing on first, second, and third base. Finally, the Identity of Oliver pitches the next book in the series, which is guaranteed to be a grand slam hit.

Chronicles of Heart and Revenge is the third book in The Identity of Oliver Series. The glitches in Oliver's profound journey through life have finally been exposed. Now all the fantastic pieces of this obscure puzzle come together to form one final enigma to solve. Oliver plans to marry his beloved, but impossible goals must be achieved before the father of the bride walks her down the aisle. These obscure tasks provided a fantastic opportunity to develop the most gripping storylines of the entire series. This leads you to embark on a sequence of anomalous adventures around the globe as Oliver is forced into the seedy underworld of black-market crimes. Prepare yourself to venture into the inner-city slums of some of the world's most dangerous places, as well as tropical islands and beautiful beaches at some of the most exotic destinations on earth. You'll travel to the Philippines, Mexico, Columbia, Switzerland, Denmark, Brazil, the Czech Republic, Costa Rica, Thailand, Nicaragua, Germany, Indonesia, Guatemala, Honduras... fourteen countries in all before Oliver finally meets his nemesis for the last time.

Author's Footnotes about West Coast Chronicles

As you read West Coast Chronicles, you will find that this novel is much different from Hometown Chronicles and Chronicles of Heart & Revenge. By design, Hometown Chronicles is the most emotional of these three novels, and Chronicles of Heart & Revenge is the most exciting. The events that occur during West Coast Chronicles are necessary to understand The Identity of Oliver Series. However, this novel was partially written simply as a bridge between the storylines of Hometown Chronicles and Chronicles of Heart & Revenge. Some chapters in West Coast Chronicles have no relation to the main storyline or plot. However, they do follow the same timeline and are entertaining to read. This provided me with an opportunity to write a couple of riveting subplots that I truly adore. I wanted to make sure my readers understood this as they read through this novel. I had a lot of fun writing this body of literature, but I believe that my best work is Hometown Chronicles and Chronicles of Heart & Revenge. This doesn't mean West Coast Chronicles won't be your favorite novel in the series. It was a wonderful story to write and it is a wonderful story to read. I hope you enjoy West Coast Chronicles as much as I do.

West Coast Chronicles is dedicated to all the people I used to party with.

I hope you are doing well.

West Coast Chronicles

Chapter I

ON THE MORNING OF July 12, 2001, I fled from my hometown of Ogallala and headed west down Interstate 70 without any destination in mind. I could have driven in any direction, and it wouldn't have made one bit of difference. My only plan was to drive as far as I possibly could before the corrupt law enforcement of Ogallala Police Department issued a warrant for my arrest. This left me roughly twenty hours of drive time before I officially became a fugitive.

I drove for two hundred and eleven miles across the flat land of Nebraska into Colorado without speeding until I reached Denver three hours later. Nearing the city, I pulled over at a truck stop to get a hotdog and refuel before continuing west on Interstate 70 into the foothills. It didn't take long before I hit the first switchback on this road through the great Rocky Mountains. My car sputtered over Loveland Pass and through the Eisenhower Tunnel before descending into the Silverthorn Valley.

I drove passed ski resorts and through snow-covered mountains for another sixty miles until I reached the city of Glenwood Springs. I stopped in this town only to fill up the gas tank in my 1989 Honda Civic. Then, I continued to drive west across the Utah border until I hit a flat stretch of road that left me nothing to do but think about why I embarked on this journey. I was on the run from corrupt law enforcement and the twisted fate of bizarre criminal misfortune. My two best friends were recently charged with murder, and I was accused of being an accomplice to these horrific crimes.

However, I wasn't on the run from these crimes per se. I was actually fleeing from a recent offer made by the Ogallala City Police Department to drop my charges if I provided statements to help convict my two best friends of the crimes they allegedly committed. If I were to accept the police department's offer, my statements would be critical to prosecuting my friends with murder. After several long hours of internal debate, I decided that I didn't want to accept this offer or answer to the crimes I was being accused of. This is why I fled town without a planned destination in mind. If I had been older, I would have likely given all this more thought and chosen a different path, but I was eighteen years old and immature at this point in my life. This was my middle finger response to corrupt law enforcement, and I had no intention of turning back.

These peculiar thoughts stuck with me all the way until I hit the intersection of Interstate 70 and Interstate 15 in the middle of Utah. At that point, I had the decision of driving north to Salt Lake City, Utah, or driving south to Las Vegas, Nevada. I had been on the run for about ten hours when I pulled into the truck stop at this intersection. My initial plans were to ditch my car around this point in time, but it was three o'clock in the morning, and this truck stop was the only building around for miles.

The last thing I wanted to do was sit around begging people for a ride at a truck stop in the middle of nowhere. I figured there was no chance of finding someone willing to pick up a hitchhiker in the middle of the night, and something about this place was giving me the creeps. My new plan was to drive south to Las Vegas and ditch my car there. This decision was based on my assumption that it would be easier for a fugitive to disappear in a place nicknamed "The City of Sin" than in a city known for conservative religious values. After microwaving a chuck wagon sandwich and filling my tank full of gas, I started to drive south on Interstate 15 toward Las Vegas.

I spent the next three hours driving down the darkest, most desolate freeway I had ever seen in my life. After being on the road for nearly twelve hours, this dark road and lack of oncoming traffic made it very difficult to stay awake. I had been listening to the same punk rock mix tape for hours and needed something new to listen to if I planned to stay awake long enough to make it to Las Vegas. So, I reached inside my center council for a different mix tape and randomly pulled out a cassette labeled "Erica's Favorite Songs #4." Rolling down the window and cranking up the volume, I hoped these songs would help me stay awake for another two hundred miles.

The first song on this mix tape was "Zombie" by the Cranberries, and the second was "Crash Into Me" by Dave Matthews. I loved both of these songs, but they did not inspire me to sing at the top of my lungs. The third song on the tape was "Making Love Out of Nothing at All" by Air Supply. The fourth was "Porcelain" by Moby, and the fifth song was "Lightning Crashes" by Live. Songs 4 and 5 started to warm my vocal cords up, but I was still hoping to hear some bangers to keep me going. The sixth song on the mix tape was "Champagne Supernova" by Oasis, and the seventh was "Creep" by Radiohead. The eighth song was "Oughta Know" by Alanis Morissette, the ninth song was "No Rain" by Blind Melon, the tenth song was "Gypsy" by Fleetwood Mac, and the eleventh was "Losing My Religion" by REM. The twelve and final song on side one was "Bullet with Butterfly Wings" by Smashing Pumpkins. I was rocking out hard before I flipped the tape over and hoped this momentum continued on the other side.

The first song on the second side of this mix tape was "Heart Shaped Box" by Nirvana, the second song was "Jane Says" by Jane's Addiction, the third song was "Black" by Pearl Jam, the fourth song was "Mr. Jones" by Counting Crows, the fifth song was "Buddy Holly" by Weezer, the sixth song was "Hey Jealousy" by Gin Blossoms. These six songs were fantastic! They were exactly what I wanted to hear. The seventh song was "Plush" by Stone Temple Pilots, and the eighth song was "Civil War" by Guns & Roses. I was singing my heart out now and was ready to listen to more. The ninth song was "Fade Into Me" by Mazzie Star, and the tenth was "Nothing Compares to You" by Sinead O'Connor. These two songs were great, but they didn't help me to stay awake at all, so I was counting on Erica's Favorite Songs #4 to knock it out of the park with the last few songs on side two. Unfortunately, the following three songs were "Just Like Heaven," "Love Song," and "Letter to Elise," all by The Cure. I wasn't expecting to hear these three songs. I wasn't prepared to listen to these three songs, and I didn't want to hear them! I should have pressed fast forward or stop, but I didn't. I just listened to the depressing melodies and lyrics without thinking. Now, I had Erica on my mind and Robert Smith's voice stuck in my head. Nothing is more upsetting than listening to The Cure with a broken heart.

Erica and I spent the past two years of our lives madly in love. It would be wonderful to describe what we experienced and how we felt during this time, but the feeling of love is fleeting, and this emotion cannot be explained. All I can tell you is that what we felt was profound and powerful. It was true love, fairy tale love, and I fucked it up... twice... now I was running away. I didn't feel good about this or anything else in my life as I traveled down that lonely stretch of highway. Every meaningful relationship that I ever had in my life was completely destroyed. I was only eighteen years old, and my heart was broken. This is what I thought about that night and what I dreamed about the night before. This is what was keeping me awake as I pressed on through the night.

Thankfully, ninety minutes had passed by the time the last song was played on the mix tape labeled "Erica's Favorite Songs #4. I only had sixty miles left to travel until I reached Las Vegas and one more hour to think about how distressing my life was. During this time, I came up with a million questions to ask the world. I thought about my family, friendships, and every minute I spent with Erica. I thought of all the promises I made and which ones were broken. I attempted to envision a future that made sense and tried to imagine being happy. I searched for a reason to live and for something to live for. This is what I wanted the world to answer. Unfortunately, I came up with nothing. I spent the rest of the drive feeling lost in the painful emotions of a broken heart, thinking this horrible feeling would never go away.

I finally arrived in Las Vegas an hour before sunrise and quickly found a place to ditch my vehicle. It took me only a few minutes to clean out all the identifying information in my cubbies and remove the license plates from my bumper. Then, I emptied my backpack and spent another few minutes taking inventory of my belongings. I found a Leatherman tool and three ballpoint pens in the front pocket. I also found one pair of shorts, two shirts, two pairs of socks, three boxer shorts, and three notebooks in the main pocket. When I repacked my backpack, there was just enough room for the shoebox full of cash I brought with me.

Thankfully, when I ditched my car, it was still dark enough for me to see the bright casino lights from the Las Vegas strip because I didn't know where anything was when I took off walking. I finally reached Las Vegas Boulevard just after 9 a.m. and was determined to book a room at the first hotel I found.

I saw a massive tower on the horizon for at least an hour before finally figuring out that I was looking at the Strat Hotel, Casino & Tower. It was approximately two miles south of Interstate 515 and was the northernmost hotel on Las Vegas Boulevard. When I finally arrived at the entrance of this hotel, I saw an advertisement for a $3.99 steak & eggs breakfast.

At this point, I hadn't eaten a good meal for at least thirty-six hours, so I filled my belly with two $3.99 steak & eggs breakfast meals. This wasn't a cure for my broken heart, and by no means was I looking at my future with a smile on my face, but it finally ended a month-long streak of persistent sadness. Now, all I needed to do was pay for a room and go to sleep. Unfortunately, this didn't go as planned because the lady at the front desk told me that a large conference had already booked all two thousand rooms in the Strat Hotel, Casino &Tower.

I was bummed out about this because this hotel looked incredible, and I really needed some sleep. I asked what was so important about this conference and why they needed to book every room in the hotel. The front desk lady told me that this was an annual, week-long conference called Male Sexual Dysfunction, and all the attendees were doctors who flew in from all parts of the world.

A woman seemed to notice my disappointment and offered me a weeklong pass to the observation tower, allowing me to visit as many times as I wanted during the week. She explained that the tower was unique because it was the second tallest in the Western Hemisphere and the tallest in the United States, with a height of 1149 feet. She also gave me a free meal token for the Top of the World restaurant, a revolving rooftop eatery situated at the very top of the tower.

I was so excited about all this that I asked if I could go up to the observation tower before I even left the hotel. She said I could go when I wanted to and encouraged me to see it. So, I immediately walked over to the elevators at the base of the tower and started my way up to the observation deck. Even the elevator was awesome because it had a speedometer showing how fast it traveled. I couldn't believe that the top speed was 1801 feet per minute. This elevator was one of three, but I made it to the observation deck in less than five minutes! Then, I spent at least an hour looking around at all the extraordinary hotels in Las Vegas. I could see every hotel in the entire city from this tower.

The Las Vegas hotels were not the only thing I saw while walking around the observation deck. I also passed by a conference room with walls of glass several times. I noticed about fifty people in this room, but I didn't think much of it until right before I decided to leave. This was when I saw a man with a boner who had some weird suction device wrapped around it. I couldn't believe what I was looking at. Then, I noticed an attractive young woman who could not have been much older than me standing about twenty feet away. She was faced toward a blank wall and seemed to be there for a reason. I hoped that she didn't see me looking at the guy with a boner. She didn't move or look away from the wall for two or three minutes. Eventually, my curiosity got the best of me, and I approached her to ask what she was thinking.

"Hi there. I was standing by the window looking at all the neat-looking hotels on the Strip, and then I noticed you staring at this wall, so I decided to come over and see what you were looking at. So, anyway, what are you looking at?" I asked.

"Nothing," the girl replied.

"Huh, I sometimes look at nothing, too, I guess. My name is Oliver. What's your name?"

"I'm Katy."

"Are you here for the conference?" I asked.

"Yeah, kind of."

"Wow, you must have a Doogie Howser brain or something."

"Why do you say that?" Katy asked with a giggle.

"Because I've never met a doctor who looked so young," I answered. "All the doctors I've ever met are old guys who smell funny."

"Funny," Katy responded with another chuckle. "What does funny smell like?"

"You know... that funky old people smell."

"Oh my God," Katy responded with a slow, belly-roll laugh." Now that's funny. Actually, I'm one of.... mmmm... maybe fifty people at this conference who are not doctors. I came with my brother."

"Is your brother a doctor?"

"Nope, he isn't a doctor either."

"What are you doing here then?"

"I'm a receptionist at a male sexual dysfunction clinic in Houston," Katy replied. "The doctor in the clinic where I work attends this conference every year. So, one day, I decided to check out the Male Sexual Dysfunction Conference Website, and I noticed that it was looking for men to demonstrate how to use erectile dysfunction equipment. I thought this was funny, so I sent it to my brother as a joke, telling him that he would be a perfect candidate... but he didn't seem to think it was a joke. Long story short, he applied for the position and was chosen to attend this conference. Once the doctor at my clinic found out about this, he asked if I wanted to come along as a guest to learn more about this profession."

"No way," I responded. "Your brother is that dude with a boner in the glass room with that weird thing wrapped around his..... umm... actually... someone told me about some guy...um that had a boner... and umm..."

"Yeah, you saw him... Huh?" Katy replied.

"No... umm... well... actually..."

"Don't lie."

"Okay... Yeah, I saw him, but in my defense... there shouldn't be a dude with a boner demonstrating how to use weird dick devices in a glass room when there are people like me walking around who just want to enjoy themselves."

This caused Katy to bust out in full-blown belly roll laughter for a solid thirty seconds before she finally caught her breath and said, "Yeah, there shouldn't even be such a thing as a glass wall meeting room... and there definitely should not be anyone in there with a boner." This caused Katy to start laughing like crazy all over again. "And for the love of God, my brother should not be in that room demonstrating how to use a fucking penis pump." Once again, she laughed and laughed. "Thanks for making my day. I needed that," Katy said, as she looked at her watch. "Well, the demonstration ended about a minute ago, so I have to head back. It was nice meeting you, Oliver."

"It was nice meeting you too," I replied, and this concluded my experience with the observation deck at the Strat Hotel, Casino & Tower. After taking the elevator down to the lobby, I stopped by the front desk to thank the lady who gave me the week-long pass and a free meal token to the Top of the World restaurant. Once I left the hotel, I started to walk toward the larger hotels on the strip with a goal of finding out if the big black pyramid I saw from the observation deck was a hotel.

Chapter II

I FELT SOMEWHAT CHEERFUL after leaving the Strat Hotel, Casino & Tower, which was a mixed emotion at the time, but it was enough to put a little grin on my face as I walked towards the Vegas Strip. I figured the black pyramid I was searching for was probably a hotel, and if so, that's where I wanted to stay. Along the way, I passed several hotels, such as Sahara Las Vegas, Circus Circus, Treasure Island, The Mirage, Caesars Palace, The Venetian, Flamingo Las Vegas, and Bellagio. I felt extremely hot during this walk, and it all made sense when I saw a thermometer reading 101 degrees. The only relief I got from the heat was when I passed by a large air-conditioned hotel or casino with its doors open.

I walked for almost an hour until I spotted the enormous black pyramid I'd been searching for. By coincidence, this was the same time that I was approached by someone about my age who offered to sell me a fake ID. I hadn't considered that I couldn't do much in Las Vegas without being twenty-one years old. The person had a convincing sales pitch and persuaded me to purchase a fake ID for one hundred dollars. So, I followed him back a few blocks along the same path I'd just come from until we arrived at the Imperial Palace Hotel. We then went to his room, and I had a fake ID within thirty minutes.

It was almost 1 pm, and I planned to head straight to the black pyramid to find out if it was a hotel. I wanted to get a room as soon as possible because I felt exhausted and hungry. However, before leaving the Imperial Palace Hotel, I noticed a sign advertising an all-you-can-eat buffet for $8.99. I decided to check it out and was amazed by the variety of food offered. This buffet table was huge! It had all different types of salads, pasta, and at least twelve different kinds of desserts. It also had all sorts of sandwiches, burgers, tacos, and burritos. There was a gigantic cheese tray and three massive towers of meat. One tower had beef, lamb, veal, pork, and sausage. The second tower had chicken, turkey, duck, goose, and even emu! The third tower had all types of seafood. There was halibut, Alaskan salmon, bluefin tuna, mussels, oysters, scallops, clams, lobster, and a big pile of crab legs!

Growing up, I ate plenty of good food because my mom was an excellent cook. There are also a lot of pheasants and cattle ranches near Ogallala, so I wasn't a stranger to good cuts of meat. However, the only seafood that I ever ate was fish caught from Lake Mc-Conaughy, and occasionally, my mom would buy Alaskan salmon or halibut for special occasions. I always heard about how good lobster and crab legs were, but I never actually had the chance to eat it. There was no way I was going to pass this opportunity up, especially for only $8.99. I couldn't believe how incredible this meal was!

To top it off, I was able to purchase my first beer with my new ID, but I didn't drink just one beer. I drank seven pints of Budweiser poured from the tap while eating three plates of seafood. I almost ate the entire pile of crab legs! I was a little drunk and felt like a king when I left the hotel restaurant. This is when I realized that I could also gamble with my new ID. I saw a few slot machines only a few feet from the front door of the restaurant, so I reached into my shorts and found a quarter. I won three dollars on this pull. Then, I put a quarter in the slot machine next to it and won seven dollars. To see if this winning streak would continue, I sat down and pulled the handle on the slot machine for another twenty minutes. In that short time, I won another twenty dollars. Considering I was up thirty bucks and just ate the best meal of my life for under ten dollars, I decided to get a room at the Imperial Palace Hotel rather than walk all the way down to the black pyramid.

Once I was handed the key to my room, I took an elevator to the nineteenth floor and slept for a few hours. After my nap, the first thing I did was count the money in the shoebox. This started as a full shoebox packed full of cash. However, before I left Ogallala, I put a substantial amount of this money in a coffee can Erica set out on the supermarket front counter where she works to raise money for her father's heart transplant. Nevertheless, I still counted out just over seventeen thousand dollars.

I put some money in my pocket, but put most of it back in the shoebox and hid it under the bed in my hotel room. After taking a cold shower, I walked down the hall looking for a soda machine and discovered that the Imperial Palace Hotel had a rooftop pool. The fact that I was staying on the top floor next to the pool without even requesting this was put in the category of good luck. I felt like I had a little streak going. My only issue now was that I didn't have swim trunks, so I went back downstairs and asked the concierge where I could buy some trunks. He said that Walmart was about eight blocks off the strip. At the age of eighteen, it didn't matter that it was over one hundred degrees outside... eight blocks wasn't very far away.

After buying some trunks, I spent an hour or two at the pool, pretending I wasn't looking at all the hot babes in tiny swimsuits. I didn't know this at the time, but I had just gotten one of the worst sunburns of my life while hanging out at this rooftop pool. However, I didn't need to deal with that quite yet. I took a nap for a few hours again after getting out of the pool and thought that since I had done well at gambling earlier, I might as well try it again that night.

In the summer of 2001, big, baggy shorts and pants were in style. It wouldn't be long before the style of baggy clothes transitioned into tight clothes, but for now, the shorts I wore were super baggy and had huge pockets. I walked down the Las Vegas strip that evening, going from one casino to the next, putting quarters into hundreds of slot machines, and it seemed like I lined up three cherries every time I pulled the handle down. By midnight, I had filled my gigantic pockets full of quarters. I walked down the Vegas strip, sounding like a giant piggy bank.

I was winning so much money that I decided to spread my gambling wings. I rolled some dice playing craps and was dealt some cards at the blackjack table. I wasn't as successful with these games as slot machines, but I don't think I lost money playing them either. With my brand new ID in my pocket, I spent all night, into the wee hours of the morning, gambling my ass off and getting absolutely shit-faced drunk.

I was so drunk that I forgot all about going to the Luxor Hotel and Casino. The moment I saw it from the Strat Hotel observation tower, I was fascinated with the big black pyramid, and I don't remember ever being there. The only reason I know that I even stepped foot through the front door was that I woke up the next morning with poker chips in my pocket with the Luxor Hotel and Casino logo on them.

Eventually, my excellent luck started to run out. My streak of good luck on the slot machines stopped, and I definitely couldn't win at craps or cards. I finally came stumbling in through the front doors of the Imperial Palace Hotel around four o'clock in the morning and brought all my quarters over to the teller. Despite losing toward the end of the night, I still had nearly three hundred dollars in quarters to cash in. That gives you an idea of how big my shorts and pockets were.

At this point, I should have just gone straight to my hotel room and gone to sleep, but right when I entered the elevator and pushed button #19, I looked over and saw a gambling game I hadn't played yet. The elevator doors closed on my arm and then opened up to new gambling possibilities. I had a goal to play every gambling game Las Vegas had to offer that night, so I stumbled over to the roulette table to try my luck. Unfortunately, this game quickly revealed that my streak of good luck didn't just end, it had run completely out.

It was my 21st birthday, according to my new ID, and oxygen was being pumped into the casinos. I was so drunk that I was seeing two of everything and could barely stand up, but my drunk ass still figured out how to play roulette. All you needed to do was pick a number or a color. The roulette dealer had the most difficult job in the casino because he had to spin the roulette wheel. If the little ball fell on your number, you were rich, and if it fell on your color, you doubled your money. Nobody could fuck this up, right?

Let me tell you, if there was a way to fuck up at a roulette table, I absolutely nailed it! At first, I lost $5, so I bet $10, thinking that if I won this time, I would break even... but I lost again. Then, I put down $30, using the same logic, and lost another time. After calculating some drunken math and my thrice-failed attempt to win a game of roulette, I put $90 on red, then $135 on black, $270 again on red, and finally $260 on black one more time. I lost $800 in less than five minutes. That was over twice the money I won playing slot machines earlier in the night. Common sense would tell a person to quit, but I was one of only a few people gambling at four in the morning, so the only casino floor bartender stood beside me with a tray filled with shots of tequila. I took five shots in five minutes and figured there was no way in hell I could lose at roulette eight times in a row, and I had only played seven times. It was perfect drunken logic with no correlation or strategy when applied to reality, but it sounded like a hell of a plan after dozens of stiff drinks.

I walked to the front desk to get a pen and paper to figure out how much money I needed to break even. Then, I started walking back to the roulette table with a drunk look on my face and $800 in my hand. At this point in the night, I had everything going for me, but I didn't get very far before my perfect plans all fell apart.

By the time the roulette dealer saw me stumbling across the casino floor, the last thirty or so shots I took that night started to kick in. I'm pretty sure he was ready to call 911 by the time I made it back over to the roulette wheel. I fell flat on my face three times, lost a shoe, and had to crawl most of the way there, but I was determined to win. "Are you sure you want to do this?" the roulette dealer asked as I put ninety-three dollars on 19 black. "You already lost a pile of money just trying to get over to the table. Look, those two old people standing behind you with smiles on their faces and a wad of cash in their hands followed you all the way here."

I was far too drunk to remember what I said to the roulette dealer, but I'm sure it was something clever and indecipherable. Just before the roulette wheel was spun, I looked around the casino, thinking I was Don Johnson. Everyone was looking at me. There were the two old people standing behind me wearing green visors, three tweakers were walking around the casino floor looking for loose change, the casino floor bartender was still handing me shots of tequila, and one guy just walked out of the bathroom with a big titty hooker. There might have even been a hotel employee mopping the floor.

When the roulette wheel started to spin, I envisioned a crowd of people cheering, bells going off, confetti falling from the ceiling, and winning so much money that the Imperial Palace Hotel would need a wheel barrel to bring it to me. The last thing I remember from that night was looking over at the roulette dealer spinning the wheel and thinking to myself, "I got you motherfucker! I'm a gambling God!"

I woke up the following morning with the worst hangover I had ever had by a long shot. I had several more hangovers like this in my life before I eventually quit drinking, but this was the worst I experienced thus far. In addition to this hangover, I was simultaneously experiencing a terrible sunburn. Everything, but my ass and nut sack was red. I looked like a drunken lobster.

The first thing I did when I crawled out of bed was walk down the hallway to the ice machine to dump a bucket of ice over my head. Then, I spent the hour looking around my room for all the money

I had won at the roulette wheel, but all I found was one shoe, two lousy quarters, and tequila-stained baggy shorts filled with regrets. I planned on leaving Las Vegas with everything but a trustworthy attorney that day, but I was barely able to get to the front desk to pay for another night at the hotel.

The following day, I wandered down to the $8.99 all-you-can-eat buffet just before check out with a sunburn, a headache, and no reason to live. After eating a plate of crab legs and drinking a big glass of Mt. Dew, I asked the front desk if someone found a size nine blue shoe with an E on the side, but nobody gave a shit about me or my lost shoe. On my way back to my room, I put my last two quarters in a slot machine and lost them both. I fucking hated Las Vegas! I would have jumped out of the nineteenth-floor window at the Imperial Palace Hotel that day, but I needed to purchase a laptop computer and buy a new pair of shoes.

I spent most of that day walking around wearing only one shoe. I looked everywhere for the things I lost at the casino the other night, but I never found my integrity or self-respect. All I found was a Pacific Sun Wear and a Best Buy store at the Rainbow Promenade Shopping Center in northwest Las Vegas.

After buying some new shoes, a laptop computer, a cellphone, and a bigger backpack to fit all this shit in, I headed straight for the Strat Hotel, Casino & Tower to cash in on my free meal token at The Top of the World. When I finally reached the revolving rooftop restaurant in the hotel's observation deck, I decided to try the T-bone and Lobster special. The steak was remarkably good. Coming from Ogallala, Nebraska, and growing up on a cattle ranch, it takes a lot to impress me when it comes to steak. But this prime-cut T-bone steak was thick, tender, and cooked perfectly. I didn't care much for the lobster. It was prepared well, but it reminded me of a fish I would sometimes catch at Lake McConaughy called Eelpout. Some people love this fish and actually call it poor man's lobster, but those people are idiots. That fish is disgusting, and so is lobster, in my opinion.

After eating dinner, I wanted to check out my new computer. The reason why I bought the laptop was so I could establish communication with the man who exploited Erica on the internet. This man offered her information about illegal heart transplants in exchange for nude pictures and videos of her just before she turned eighteen years old. I planned to find this man to seek revenge. I called this person my nemesis. This was the first serious goal that I ever had in my life. My second goal was to raise enough money for a heart transplant for Erica's father.

I was able to book a room at Strat Hotel, Casino & Tower that night because the conference for male sexual dysfunction was finished. I spent the rest of that night on the dark web, researching more about my nemesis, and made some headway. I thought I knew how to contact him but needed a good reason because I figured to have only one shot at meeting this evil person to seek revenge. This was also the first time I thought about harvesting the marijuana field back at Billy's farm. I fled Ogallala's corrupt law enforcement, not considering how much money the weed in that field could be worth. For all I knew, it may have been worth a million dollars.

I thought that if I had any shot at harvesting this marijuana, then I would need to get in touch with my friend Fredrick. This was the man I went to the Phish concert with after graduating high school. I remembered our time together on the West Coast earlier in the summer. Two things about this man stuck out in my memory. The first one was that he seemed to give zero fucks about getting caught with drugs. The second was that he seemed to have some profound connections to buying and selling large quantities of weed. If my plans were set in motion, this person could help me solve a few problems of the hundreds I seemed to be facing. I had his number, so he was the first person I tried to call with my new cellphone. Unfortunately, I couldn't get in touch with him. Nevertheless, it felt like I made minor steps in the right direction that night when putting my two goals into perspective.

To conclude my stay in Las Vegas, I checked out the next day and once again returned to the epic $8.99 buffet all-you-can-eat buffet at the Imperial Palace. There wasn't much I would miss about this city, but this buffet would undoubtedly be at the top of my list of the few things I enjoyed. Later that afternoon, I found my way to a truck stop outside town. I kind of figured hitchhiking would be straightforward. However, I discovered that people aren't super excited to let a random eighteen-year-old ride with them toward wherever they may be headed. After looking at a map, I figured I would be headed to Los Angeles to find Fredrick, but the world had different plans for me.

After two hours of asking everyone who stopped at the truck stop if I could catch a ride headed west, the only person willing was someone named Jed, who was on his way to Salt Lake City, Utah. I asked a person to give me a ride who was wearing cotton dockers, just like from a famous commercial in the 90's. After so many failed attempts at hitchhiking until this point, I was just happy to be getting a ride. I wasn't stoked about going to Salt Lake City, but I had not been there before, so it would be a new experience. It just happened to be in the opposite direction I thought I would be headed. I slept most of the way to Salt Lake City. The little conversation I had with this person made me realize I was traveling with someone a little off.

"Hey, wake up," Jed said.

"Holy shit, what's up?" I answered.

"I live in a village outside of Salt Lake City about ten miles," Jed replied. "I want to stop there to get something to eat. Then, I will bring you the rest of the way to Salt Lake City."

"Okay, whatever," I answered, immediately falling back to sleep.

I was in the strangest village of people ever when I woke up. The men were all dressed exactly like Jed, and the women were all dressed alike, wearing dresses down to their ankles.

"Wait here, and duck down," Jed said, as we pulled up in front of what I figured to be his parent's house and where he lived. Approximately thirty minutes later, Jed returned with a meal for me. This consisted of chicken, potatoes, carrots, and weird desserts. "Stay down till after we drive out of my village," Jed said. "Here is some food." Although the food he gave me was absolutely disgusting, I ate it anyway because I was so hungry. After a few minutes, Jed said, "Okay, now you can sit up."

"What the hell was that all about?" I asked.

"Religious matters," Jed replied. "Where do you want to be dropped off in Salt Lake City?"

"I guess downtown," I replied, feeling oddly satisfied that the village we had just visited was nearly identical to what I pictured a Mormon village to look like. For reasons that are hard to explain, I was happy about this random chance to have caught a ride with an over-the-top Mormon. At least, I think Jed was a Mormon. I never did ask him the specifics about his religious matter. It's just my best guess. Anyway, about a half hour later, I was dropped off downtown.

"Thanks for the ride," I said.

"No problem," Jed replied. "Good luck with the rest of your travels."

I was dropped off right in the middle of downtown across the street from a bar, so I decided to go inside to ponder my next move. However, I learned from a guy standing at the front door that Salt Lake City has these weird laws that force you to purchase a membership to enter any establishment that serves beer or liquor. This didn't appeal to me, so I asked him to call me a cab, which took me to the biggest truck stop in Salt Lake City. About ten minutes later, I was dropped off at a truck stop with all sorts of semi-trucks refueling. This truck stop was great because it had awesome hotdogs and other gas station food. It was also on the edge of town, offering a great mountain view.

After about an hour, I was super lucky and got a ride from a semi-truck driver. He said he was headed to Portland, Oregon, which was fine with me. After we both showered at this rest stop, we climbed inside his 18-wheeler. Coincidentally, this man's semi-truck was a mid-roof sleeper, just like the two trucks my dad owned.

"Since we will be traveling together for several hundred miles, I suppose we should introduce ourselves," the truck driver said. "My name is Big Ed, but some call me Eddie. What is your name, young man?"

"My name is Oliver," I answered.

"Oliver... huh? Well, that will be easy to remember because that is my nephew's name," Big Ed replied, "So, may I ask what you are doing hitchhiking?"

"I just graduated from high school and wanted to go on an adventure, I guess."

"Was it your intention to go to Portland or are you headed that way now since that is where my destination is?"

"A little bit of both," I answered. "Do you wanna know what is interesting?"

"What's that?" Big Ed asked.

"My dad used to drive a mid-roof sleeper like this one."

"Is he retired now?"

"No, he leases a couple of trucks identical to this and has a couple of guys that drive for him sometimes. Or at least, I think that's what is going on. I don't pay much attention to what he does these days. In any case, he is trying to get me to become a truck driver. However, my mom doesn't like that because she wants me to go to college." I answered.

"So, what do you want to do?" Big Ed asked.

"I must admit, I'm not entirely sure myself," I replied. "If I did know, then I probably wouldn't have to rely on the kindness of truck drivers to get around. Please don't take offense, and thank you so much for picking me up. The last time I waited a long time to get a ride, so I am very grateful for it."

"It sounds like you have a good family," Big Ed replied. "Do you think you might go to college after you finish adventuring?"

"Maybe," I replied. "I am certainly keeping those cards on the table."

"It sounds like if you don't go to college, you may wind up becoming a truck driver like your father and me."

"It's possible," I replied, as this conversation faded into about an hour of silence. I started to drift off into sleep, which was relatively easy to accomplish, considering I had so little solid rest the past several days. I was awakened at some point by Big Ed, who generously offered to let me sleep in his bed. I was excited to take him up on his offer and get some rest. However, at some point, he kicked me out so he could sleep himself.

Chapter III

WE PULLED OVER AT a giant truck stop in Boise, Idaho, for a solid eight hours so Big Ed could sleep. During this time, I just sat around the truck stop, taking several breaks to smoke weed. I asked several people where they were going and tried to procure a ride instead of hanging out doing nothing for eight hours. Unfortunately, there were no connections that made sense, so I wound up just hopping back in with Big Ed and continuing onward. The following day, I saw Mt. Hood as we were approaching the city of Portland, Oregon, and we arrived at a truck stop on the outskirts of town around noon. After saying goodbye to Big Ed, I asked the truck stop clerk to call me a cab.

I wandered around Portland for the next several hours, looking for a cheap hotel that was close to downtown. I thought I'd try to be more of a spendthrift moving forward. I had no idea how long I would need to live on this cash, and I also spent a pretty sizable wad in Vegas. The place I found was called Motel 9. It was attempting to be Motel 6's stupid cousin or something. This place was an absolute dump. Not only was the bed hard, and TV not hooked up to cable, it appeared to be a magnet for hookers and drug addicts. The motel advertised Wi-Fi, but I could never get it to work.

For the next few days, I spent a lot of time drinking coffee inside Starbucks. Unfortunately, this was really one of the only public places that had Wi-Fi, but as long as I had money to buy coffee, I could sit in the corner of Starbucks all day long. I spent my time at the coffee shop searching the dark web, learning everything I could about my nemesis. At this point, I could have contacted this evil man anytime, but I didn't want to make a mistake and scare him. I guessed that I would have something figured out soon. I also started to transfer some of my writing over to my laptop. Up until now, I have just written in a notebook. I found using a computer to be much better than scribbling in a notebook, particularly because I needed to push a button to erase a word rather than scribble it out.

This Starbucks sat on the corner near a pizza place and a local tavern in a neighborhood that looked like it was constructed early in the twentieth century. The sidewalks were made of enormous blocks of stone rather than concrete. Giant trees were growing everywhere I looked, and the houses on this street were gigantic. At first, I thought I must be in a rich part of Portland. Then, I noticed the cars parked on the street in front of these houses. I was confused as to why so many shitty vehicles were parked in front of what I thought to be mansions.

As I walked towards downtown, I took a closer look at the houses. I was amazed to see that they were much larger than any house in my hometown. At the end of the block, I noticed a mailman emptying mail from a giant blue mailbox. I stopped at the corner momentarily, feeling a little confused about the neighborhood. I watched the mailman finish pulling out the last mail from the mailbox before approaching him to ask a few questions.

"Hey, I was just wondering... do wealthy families live in these houses?" I asked with a curious and sincere expression.

The mailman looked at me with a cigarette dangling out of his mouth while he fumbled through his pockets. After pulling out some matches to light his cigarette, he crossed his brow and looked at me from the corner of his eye, "What in the hell are you talking about?" the mailman asked.

"Do wealthy families live in this neighborhood?" I asked again.

"I live two blocks that way in a basement apartment, so if you consider mailmen to be rich, I guess so," the mailman answered with a smirk.

"How much does it cost to rent houses like the ones on this block?" I asked.

"If you were to rent all the apartments inside one of these modified mansions," the mailman answered, "it would probably run you a few grand or so. I know a two-bedroom apartment around here is probably pretty nice for around six hundred dollars, and I plan to live in it soon. In less than a year, I will stop paying my piece of shit ex-wife child support, and on that day, I will have one hell of a smile on my face."

"No shit," I replied, now fully realizing that rich people did not own these giant houses.

"What?' the mailman asked.

"Ahh... Nothing, I was just wondering because I was maybe thinking of renting a place around here, that's all."

"Welcome to the neighborhood. I will probably be your mail carrier if you rent an apartment here. If that day ever comes, and you experience problems with your rent check being delivered on time, you can probably assume that it was lost in the mail," the mailman said, as he chuckled at his lame joke and walked away.

After walking down a few streets, I stood at a busy intersection, crossing a road toward downtown. From this place, I could see a park and an excellent view of the buildings above everything around me. Several large trees stood between me and these buildings. Continuing toward downtown, I decided to stop at the park for a few minutes to admire the view. Looking down at a sidewalk that stretched through the middle of the park, I saw all sorts of people. The trees were much different than the trees in Nebraska and also much different than the trees near the ocean. When I looked to the southeast, I could see the summit of Mt. Hood covered in snow.

The park itself brushed against the center of the city. Just to the right of Mt. Hood, I saw the tops of a few skyscrapers from where I stood. A clear view of the skyline wasn't visible through all the trees, so I began walking off toward the edge of the park, where a large grass field was. I crossed this field to get a clear view of downtown Portland. Looking around, the tall buildings captivated me. After living in a small town in the middle of nowhere my whole life, it felt refreshing to see something different. I mean, Las Vegas and Venice Beach were different, but not in a homey way like this.

As I approached the road between the park and the tall buildings, I found it rather strange as I watched an older man with a cane cross the street very slowly without anyone to help him. Of all the things I could think about while standing in that park, I wondered what old people felt like living in a city of this size. All sorts of people passed this man as they crossed the same street, and I seemed to be the only one who even noticed that he walked amongst half a million people in this city who were younger than him.

Although he took much smaller steps and moved slowly, he eventually crossed the street. Then, he turned down the walkway in the direction of downtown Portland. I now felt inspired to go downtown and walk passed him with an enthusiastic stride. After about a minute, I saw this man disappear behind a large red bus, which I quickly realized was likely headed downtown. I ran toward a crowd of people who had been waiting for the bus to arrive but didn't quite make it. I had not taken a public bus before and added this to the short list of things I planned to do that day.

I was confident that a bus would bring me downtown much faster than my enthusiastic stride, but I was young, so walking didn't seem a chore so much as an adventure. As I approached downtown, I noticed some unique structures that stood out from the trees and buildings. An accurate description of these structures seemed lost within an enigma of modern architecture. Unlike the many colors and designs that created the buildings all around me, the purpose of this peculiar structure remained a mystery to me for several minutes.

It wasn't until I stood at the very foot of one of these structures that I realized I was standing at the entrance of the Portland Art Museum. I initially thought admission to this museum was free. However, after I entered through the front entrance, I saw that it would cost me ten dollars, which I would try to avoid paying. I tried to explain to an elderly lady collecting money at the front door that I was an art student from Nebraska and wanted to use the experience of entering this art museum for a term paper I was writing.

"I applaud your dedication to art if you have decided to take a summer course to study this museum," she replied. "All I need is your school ID, young man, and I will have no problem with you looking around the museum to help you with your studies."

"Dang! I think I forgot my ID in Nebraska," I said, after fishing through an empty bag of excuses.

"You have to pay the ten-dollar entrance fee," the elderly woman replied.

"Ahhh... man, but I don't have ten dollars," I replied, ironically keeping over ten grand in cash tucked inside my backpack.

"Then you can't get in," the elderly woman replied.

As I turned around toward the door to exit the building, I was stopped by a man much younger than the woman collecting money. This man seemed to be a manager of some sort and must have thought that my situation was incredibly humorous for some reason. He stood there laughing as he told me, "The Art Museum is free for the next hour."

I didn't ask any questions about why he was laughing or why the museum was free for this particular hour on a weekday afternoon. I just took it for what it was worth and walked into the Portland Art Museum with a smile on my face.

The art I saw inside this museum was much different than I expected. I saw all sorts of art created over a thousand years ago. The art that I was particularly interested in was the paintings on the third floor. Many of these pieces were from the Renaissance era. Many of these paintings seemed to be of something plain yet created for good reason. There certainly was much to ponder while admiring the unbridled talent of all these old-ass painters.

After about an hour or so, I eventually left feeling somewhat perplexed about my overall judgment of the Portland Art Museum. I had never been to an art museum before, so the surroundings naturally captivated me. However, I thought most of the art I saw that day lacked something. I had no idea what this something was, but it was needed to transcend beyond my mediocre opinion of the place. Nevertheless, it was free, which made it all marvelous to look at.

When I left the Portland Art Museum, it was about five o'clock. This was when I decided I needed to return to my hotel room to drop off my backpack. I wanted to return downtown that night and play pool in a tavern. I had it in my head that I could likely hustle some people for cash. I was eighteen and had an unusual talent for the pool game, so it made some sense, at least in theory.

This was when I found my opportunity to experience public transportation for the first time. I wasn't paying attention to what I was doing on the first bus that I got onto. Since it looked like it was headed down the street that I took to get downtown, I just figured that it would bring me back to Starbucks, where I had been using the Wi-Fi for the last few days. Unfortunately, my assumptions were dead wrong. After only a few blocks, the bus took a left and was now pointed in a direction nowhere near where I had intended to go. I then ran up to the front of the bus to ask the bus driver where the bus was going. He said it goes toward the stadium, turns around in the highlands, and returns downtown.

I told him I intended to continue down the street we had just turned off. He said that I should have gotten on the 12 or the 12L, but I could get off at the next stop and walk back six or seven blocks to catch either one of these two buses. I followed his advice, and about a half hour later, I was let off near the Starbucks, about eight blocks from my motel.

After dropping off my backpack, I immediately turned around and walked back toward Starbucks. I ended up stopping at the tavern across the street from Starbucks. I ordered a beer, and the bartender didn't think twice about my fake ID. I hadn't yet gotten used to factiously being twenty-one years old, so I thought this was still pretty cool. Anyway, I tried to play some pool there as this tavern had two nice pool tables. However, a couple were playing at one table and not really taking the game seriously, and at the other table, I plugged several quarters in, hoping that someone would want to play me. I had no such luck, so I eventually asked the bartender to call me a cab to go downtown again.

I walked around downtown for an hour or so, poking my head into bars that looked like they may have had a pool table. Then, eventually, I ended up outside a concert venue with a bunch of punk rockers. I looked up at the sign, which read, "8 pm Propagandi with opening band I-Spy." I liked punk rock bands like NOFX, Green Day, Social Distortion, Bad Religion, and Face to Face, but I was not familiar with Propagandi or I-Spy.

After talking to some punk rock kids waiting to get in, I was assured that this concert would be awesome. The music was described as skateboard punk rock, so I stood in line myself, hoping that I would be able to get a ticket to the box office. I ended up getting in line just in the nick of time because there were only a few people behind me who got in. The show was sold out.

It turns out that the advice I took from the punk rockers was right on! These guys absolutely ruled. There was one song that was played called "Anti-Manifesto" that had the entire place going nuts.

There was a mosh pit that I jumped into a few times. I was so stoked to be at this concert. This was the only concert I had attended besides when Erica and I talked our folks into letting us drive to an Elton John concert in Denver during our senior year. This was no Elton John concert. These guys were incredibly pissed off and played one hell of a show!

As I was leaving the concert venue, I ran into a kid about my age. He approached me and tried to sell me a homemade copy of a magazine he had written. "Hey man, would you buy a copy of my zine?" he asked. "I'm a writer, and I try to sell these little magazines to people hoping to get enough money for a hotel. It would really help me out. This is really my only source of income at the moment."

"What is it about?"I asked.

"It's called <u>Adam's Apple</u>," he said. My name is Adam, and this zine explains some of my challenges."

"What kind of challenges do you write about?" I asked, curious and impressed by this kid's homemade magazine.

"I'm gay if you haven't already noticed. I have known I was gay since I was in grade school. However, I didn't come out of the closet till I was fourteen. When I did this, I was made fun of by all sorts of evil classmates. I ended up getting tormented, and so did my friends for about a year. Then, to make matters worse, my dad couldn't handle me being gay and basically kicked me out of the house when I was fifteen years old. I have been on the streets ever since."

"How old are you now?" I asked, feeling incredibly sorry for him.

"I'm eighteen," he answered, handing me a copy of his magazine. "Anyway, I am selling them for one dollar. Would you maybe want to buy a copy? I only need to sell eight more to pay for a room at the motel down the street."

"Of course," I replied, and handed him a five-dollar bill from my pocket. When Adam started fumbling through his pockets for change, I said, "Keep the extra four bucks, Buddy. Hopefully, you find a place to stay tonight."

I stood there reading Adam's magazine for a while as he attempted several other sales pitches to the punk rockers still standing around after the concert. I saw that he was an excellent writer and that what he had told me was sincere. This is when I approached Adam and asked if he wanted to return to my motel for the night. I had a double bedroom, and one of the beds would not get used. He accepted my offer and must have thanked me a hundred times as we took the bus back toward the motel. Adam had mass transportation dialed and navigated a transfer onto a bus that nearly dropped us off at the front entrance of Motel 9.

Adam left early the morning after thanking me for my hospitality about fifty more times. I read the rest of Adam's self-made magazine after he left. His life was really tragic. I couldn't believe what I had read. This made me think of my life and particularly Billy's life. I experienced some sad and tragic things in my life too, but they were entirely different than what Adam experienced. I started to think that maybe I had something I could tell the world in a homemade magazine.

For the next few days, I spent a lot of time writing and drawing pictures for a magazine I was planning to make. I also organized several of my best poems and entered them into my computer. I spent most of this time at Starbucks and in some parks that I had found between Motel 9 and downtown Portland. In the end, I created a name and a cover for my zine, which I called "<u>My Writes</u>."

I found a Kinkos copy center to print ten copies of <u>My Writes</u> once it was completed, and then I tried to look for a good place to sell them to people passing by. After an hour of wandering aimlessly around downtown Portland, I eventually saw a large gathering of people in a city park. As I walked over to see what it was about, I found out that it was a political gathering, and this was when a pretty girl about my age approached me.

"Are you registered to vote?" the pretty girl asked.

"No," I replied.

"Are you eighteen years of age?"

"Yes."

"I am trying to get young people registered to vote," she said enthusiastically.

"Okay," I replied.

"Would you like to become a registered voter?"

"Sure," I responded, not because I actually wanted to be a registered voter. I honestly wouldn't care what I was registering for at this point. The fact was that this girl was drop-dead gorgeous. She had curly blond hair with a complexion that rivaled any supermodel on the planet. I was just happy to be talking to a pretty girl. She was wearing a pair of Levi's that appeared to be painted onto her legs and ass, and then she had a tee shirt all twisted up, showing off her stomach, which read, "Rock the Vote!"

"Are you a resident of Oregon?" she asked.

"No."

"Mmm... that is too bad," the pretty girl responded. "I can only get you registered to vote if you are a citizen living in Oregon."

"That sucks!" I replied. "What the hell are you voting for anyway? Isn't it a few more years before the next presidential election?"

"There are many things we are trying to get on the next ballot," the pretty girl replied. "Once Eddie finishes his speech, you can ask him about the issues we are campaigning for."

"Who is Eddie?" I asked.

"He is that guy over there standing on top of the picnic table, babbling about his political beliefs," the pretty girl said, as she pointed over to a man wrapped up in what appeared to be the American flag. He also had a long white beard strapped to his chin and wore a top hat. I listened briefly to what this man was yelling through a bullhorn.

"In 1974, Richard Nixon told the United States, "I am not a crook." That was a lie! In 1989, George Bush, Sr. told the United States, "No new taxes." That was an absolute lie! In 1999, Bill Clinton told the United States, "I did not engage in sexual relations with my intern." That was a lie! Now that we have George Bush, Jr. in office, I can assure you that we will have to listen to four years of lie after lie after lie."

"Should I be listening to what this guy is saying?" I asked the pretty girl.

"Absolutely," she answered.

"Why is that?"

"Because I can tell that you are a Democrat," she said with a smile. Then, timed with a wink, she added, "A sexy Democrat."

I didn't have any response to this, mainly because I was tongue-tied and left experiencing a full-body blush at this point. I had never thought about voting before and never really thought much about politics. However, this girl's smile alone convinced me to become a Democrat. I had no idea what being a Democrat meant, but at least for that sunny summer day, I aligned with the politics discussed in that park. As the beautiful girl continued to mingle amongst the crowd, I started listening to what the patriotic man standing on the picnic table was yelling about.

"In 1776, Thomas Jefferson told our nation that our government was created for the people, by the people. Because of this statement, and many others made during his career as a politician, I believe that this man was the best president the citizens of the United States of America have ever elected. I can only hope future presidents will state their words with integrity."

"Thomas Jefferson was a fucking racist, you political goon!" I heard someone yell out from the crowd of people. However, this heckle didn't interrupt his speech as he continued.

"We need to elect a president with the balls to tell the American people the truth. I want a president that tells America, hell yeah, I smoked pot in college! Once I become president, this will no longer be an issue, but I'm not here to discuss my personal life because that is my own damn business! I'm here to discuss politics! This is why I have brought a pie chart and a bar graph here to show you all how our government is screwing us. I have also taken it upon myself to build a PowerPoint presentation showing all the lies you've been told, the scandals you aren't supposed to know about, and the shady politics our political leaders use to get elected. Most importantly, it will show you pictures of the asses I'm going to kick once I become president.

Don't let the Democratic and Republican parties spend your tax dollars digging up dirt on me because even if it is true, I am not ashamed to tell you that the content of my character was developed by living the life of an ordinary citizen of the United States of America! I may drink and smoke a little too much sometimes. I also use foul language from time to time. I might even hang out at some seedy joints with my friends on the weekends, but if the flag still stands for freedom, damn it, you can't hold it against me! I tell you the truth because I have no reason to lie! The truth is that I am an honest, hardworking, and upstanding citizen of the United States of America. Aside from my kick-ass political views, bitchin' foreign policies, and my righteous plan for homeland security, there is a much greater reason I am running for president, and that is to bring justice to all!

I was born and raised in this great country for one reason, and that reason is to live the life of an American. I feel that it is my duty to bring this great country back to the basics by placing the Declaration of Independence in the heart and mind of every citizen living in this great country. God, as my witness, I plan to rewrite the constitution with the handwriting of our republic and let every American sign their name twice! Once, to accept the challenges of a greater nation, and twice, to remind the United States government who this country belongs to!

I don't want to live in a country whose Bill of Rights gives the right for our government to take your dollar bill away from you. I want to live in a country whose Bill of Rights wants to put one righteous dollar bill in your pocket just for doing what you think is right. I have used my freedom of speech here today to urge you to use your freedom of choice wisely. Cast your ballot, and vote for a better tomorrow! The next time our nation's children pledge allegiance to the flag, I want you to be rest assured that you belong to the republic for which it stands. Ladies and gentlemen, I am rallying for your liberty, freedom, and justice for all. God bless America!

Most people clapped as this man's speech ended. I sat around a little longer, smoking a joint with a few kids, and then asked if they wanted to buy a zine or two. I was pretty happy to find out that they all wanted one. They were likely just being nice, but it made me feel good about myself. After this, I started walking up to people at this demonstration with an unpolished sales pitch, and I sold the rest of what I had. I only printed ten copies, not thinking that this would create a viable income, which I was right about, but it was at least worth my time and effort.

What had turned into somewhat more of an income was hustling pool at a place called the Paramount in downtown Portland. This establishment had two parts. One part was a restaurant with a huge rectangular bar in the middle of it. The other part was a big room with four pool tables. Shortly after arriving in Portland, I started to spend almost every night there playing pool. Several outstanding pool players would come to this establishment to play each other for money.

I walked out of the Paramount with twenty to thirty dollars in my pocket most nights. I initially had every intention of moving on to another city, but these games kept me from leaving Portland for another solid week. I continued to stay at the shithole, Motel 9, until I really couldn't take it anymore. Seeing that I was making money most nights playing pool and selling zines during the day, I was able to justify paying for a nicer room at a Holiday Inn. This hotel was closer to downtown. I also had an indoor pool, a hot tub, a small bar, a restaurant, and Wi-Fi.

Shortly after moving my temporary residence in Portland to the Holiday Inn, I remember playing a pool game against a guy at the Paramount for ten bucks. All the balls were off the table except for the eight ball, and I was left with an almost impossible shot. If I missed this shot, I was nearly certain that I would lose the game, but that didn't happen. I hit this ball with perfect precision, and it hugged the rail all the way into the corner pocket.

"Holy shit! I can't believe that ball actually went in," I said, turning toward my opponent. "It looks like you owe me ten bucks!" This caused the guy, who I was playing against, to lose his goddamned mind! I looked at him for about ten seconds as his face turned nearly purple. I saw him grit his teeth, and suddenly, he grabbed the eight ball out of the corner pocket and held it up like he planned to throw it at me.

He didn't throw the ball at me as I anticipated. Instead, he chased me around the bar while holding this ball up like he planned to hit me with it. He chased me around the large rectangle bar several times before some random person finally tackled him. I was thankful that this man dealt with him so I didn't have to.

I wasn't running from this guy because I was scared of him. The reason I was running away from him rather than dealing with him myself was that I didn't want to get tangled up with the police. I still thought that I was a fugitive of some possible felonies, and I assumed that chasing someone around with a pool ball in your hand was illegal. I have no idea what happened to this guy after I left, but I decided that would be the last night I would stay in Portland.

Chapter IV

After leaving the Paramount, I returned to my hotel, grabbed a bite to eat at the restaurant, and then went up to my room and thought about calling Erica. It was 6 pm Pacific Time, so it was 8 pm in Ogallala. I tried to think about what I planned to say and prepare myself if Erica picked up the phone. I only spoke to her briefly a couple of times since we attended the party to celebrate the morbidly obese man's life after his funeral. After several minutes of thinking through my legal issues and a loose definition of infidelity, I finally decided to call Erica with my new cell phone.

"Hello," Erica answered.

"Hi Erica," I replied. "How are you doing?"

"That is a loaded question, Oliver."

"Yeah, I suppose that it is," I replied.

"You suppose, huh?" Erica answered. "Let me tell you how I'm doing. For starters, my dad is still dying. My brother is still stationed in the most dangerous place on earth. Two of our best friends are being charged with murder. My dad's hospital bills are piling up. If it weren't for a generous donation to my coffee can at work, I wouldn't be able to afford food for us. One more thing about how I'm doing... Oliver, what am I forgetting?" Erica asked, with a sarcastic tone in her voice. "What could that possibly be?"

"I'm sorry."

"You're sorry, huh?" Erica answered. "Oh yeah, your pathetic apology just reminded me that you had sex with a football player's girlfriend, and not just any old football player... it had to be the star quarterback's girlfriend. I bet it must have felt great having sex with the most popular girl in high school. I bet it felt almost as good as running away from your legal issues. I have no idea where the hell you are, Oliver. I'm mad at you, and I'm here alone," Erica said, as she began to cry.

"Don't cry," I responded.

"What do you expect me to do, Oliver? I am not happy. In fact, I'm downright miserable. Do you have any idea how weird things are right now?"

"What do you mean?" I asked.

"You freaked the hell out of your parents!"

"How so?" I asked.

"Your dad went down to the police station a couple of days after you went missing and threatened to beat the shit out of everyone in the entire police station. He nearly got in a brawl with like six police officers."

"I bet one of them was Deputy James O'Hare. That was the asshole that wanted me to rat out Adam and Billy. I'd love to see my dad beat that guy's ass!" I replied. "Then what happened?"

"Your dad ended up going to jail for thirty days."

"You are kidding me!" I replied. "Didn't my mom bail him out?"

"From the rumors and gossip going around, he just wanted to sit in jail and get it over with."

"Is he in jail right now?"

"As far as I know," Erica said. "and that isn't even the weirdest thing about your parents."

"What could be weirder than my dad threatening to beat up the entire police department?"

"You know how your mom is like a superwoman. She's in charge of all the events down at the church. She runs the town craft sale. She has the nicest yard in town because of all the flowers she plants, and she somehow organizes enough people to decorate the city park with Christmas shit every year."

"Yes, Erica, I know my mom pretty well."

"Your mom went batshit crazy, too!"

"Really, how?" I asked, incredibly puzzled.

"From what I've been told, she got together with her friend, Beth Iverson, at the Ogallala Post and took out a full-page ad in the newspaper! She wrote a crazy ass story about Billy, Adam, and you. She said that the police planted drugs out in the field where you were found the night of the accident and that you were trying to get Billy to pull over. She said you had nothing to do with anything related to Billy or Adam's arrest."

"No way... really?"

"That's not all," Erica said. "Your mom also explained how the police tried to get you to rat on Billy and Adam, or else they were going to charge you with crimes that you didn't commit. She has the whole goddamned town all pissed off at the police. Oliver, I'm not even sure if you are even being charged with anything anymore. I guess two police officers went to church last Sunday, and nobody would even sit within twenty feet of them. From what I understand, they dropped the charges against you later that afternoon."

"No way... really?" I answered. "Who told you this?"

"Your mom called me," Erica said. "I can call her back this afternoon to make sure, but that is the last I heard."

"Wow, that's nuts!" I said. "My parents do the weirdest shit sometimes."

"Your whole family does weird shit, Oliver. You are the weirdest one of all."

"My youngest sister isn't all that weird," I said.

"Yeah, she is pretty normal, I guess, but the rest of you are the weirdest fuckers I know!" Erica replied. "Where are you right now?"

"I'm sitting in a hotel room in Portland, Oregon."

"Portland, huh?"

"How is Billy doing?" I asked.

"Not well, from what I understand. I heard that he cracked his skull, and bones from his nose got pushed up into his brain. I think he also may have broken his neck, but that is what I just heard from Sherly, so I don't know if it is true."

"What about the family in the minivan?"

"Oh, you don't even want to know," Erica answered. "There is something on the news about them every single night. There was even an interview with the two little girls the other night. They were crying about their dad being broken and how their mom was in heaven. It was the saddest thing I ever saw ever... ever... ever... in my whole fucking life, Oliver."

"For Christ's sake," I replied. "Is anything else ever on TV?"

"Not lately. You and your goddamned friends and family are like a real-life soap opera," Erica said. "If Billy lives through all this, he isn't ever getting out of jail. According to the news, he tried to kill the happiest damn family on the planet. Adam's in prison for murdering a guy who set the world record for eating the most hotdogs. Your mom is taking out full-page ads in the newspaper and making the whole town pissed off. Your dad tried to beat the shit out of the entire police department, and you're just an idiot! The whole damned town turned into a freakshow mess!"

"Is it really that bad?"

"It's worse!" Erica replied. "I'm fucking lonely."

"Does this mean that you forgive me?" I asked.

"No," Erica answered. "It just means that I am lonely."

"Will you ever forgive me?" I desperately asked.

"Maybe," Erica answered. "That depends."

"On what?" I asked.

"If you are going to be a douchebag and cheat on me again," Erica said.

"I thought you broke up with me," I said. "I don't even know that girl's name."

"Her name is Julie, and guess what, Oliver?"

"What?" I asked.

"Julie and I had a nice long chat when she came into the super-market the other day."

"Really?"

"Yep... really," Erica replied. "She said that you tried to put your dick where it doesn't belong... but I'm over that now."

"You are?" I asked, surprised as hell.

"Yeah, I got over it the same night I found out you fucked around with Julie."

"You did?" I asked. "Why didn't you tell me? I have been going nuts thinking about you. I was crying my eyes out that night."

"I was too, Oliver, but Tyler cheered me up."

"Who the hell is Tyler?" I asked.

"That tall kid with the cool hair that drives that big red truck," Erica replied. "He saw me crying and feeling miserable when I was walking home after you got the shit kicked out of you at that party. Maybe it was because I was vulnerable, or maybe it was because I was super pissed off at you, or it could have just been because I was feeling horny, I guess. Honestly, I'm not sure why I told him to drive that big red truck of his out in the country somewhere so I could suck him off."

"You are kidding me, right?" I answered, not knowing if Erica was joking or if I was going to have to beat the shit out of someone.

"I'm not kidding, Oliver, and do you know what else?"

"What?" I asked.

"Tyler's dick is fucking huge!"

"Oh, Christ... did you really have to tell me that?"

"No," Erica answered, "but that is what you get for fucking around with Julie and then lying to me about how you just felt her tits. You are lucky you didn't have sex with her, Oliver, because guess who picked me up and took me to the movies last night?"

"I'm going to kill that son of a bitch!" I answered.

"That's going to be pretty hard to do if you're in Portland."

"So, are you and Tyler going out now?" I asked.

"Mmmmm... maybe... I did happen to rub his giant dick during the entire movie last night," Erica replied. "Then, I went with him in his big truck out into the country again. He was such a gentleman. He opened doors for me. He said "please" and "thank you." Then, he licked my asshole and covered my tits with cum. You should have been there, Oliver, it was so romantic... so what was your question again? I'm sorry, I was thinking about Tyler's cock?"

"Are you going out with that son of a bitch?"

"I guess it would depend on your plan, Oliver."

"I plan on beating the ever-living shit out of Tyler! That's what I plan to do."

"Don't even think about it!" Erica said. "If you think our relationship is on the rocks now, it can get worse... trust me... it can get a lot worse. You screwed up, Oliver! We went two years being faithful to each other and didn't have sex with anyone, including each other. That takes a lot of commitment. We were gonna get married someday. You screwed up everything! Now look at us."

"I still love you more than anything else in this entire world, Erica, and I still want to marry you," I replied with a sigh of desperation.

"I love you more than anything else in this world, too, Oliver, and I also want to marry you."

"You do?" I asked, suddenly feeling a giant wave of relief over my entire body.

"Yes, but let me tell you something... you are going to remember this conversation for the rest of your fucking life!"

"No shit," I replied, wholeheartedly agreeing with her.

"I want to make one thing crystal clear before we get off the phone tonight."

"What's that?" I asked.

"When you come back home from doing whatever the hell you are doing... I'm going to own your cock! You'll be lucky if I even let you touch it!" Erica said, with bitter words. "Do you understand what I just got done telling you?"

"Yes, I do."

"Good, 'cause if you ever fuck up like this again... the closest you'll ever get to having sex with me will be a Polaroid picture with Tyler's giant dick in my mouth."

"I swear to God, when I return home, I will never leave your side again."

"Okay," Erica said. "I'll be waiting."

"In the meantime, are we back together?"

"Nope!"

"Nope, what do you mean... nope?" I asked, feeling confused.

"I mean fucking nope, Oliver!" Erica replied with strong conviction. "When you are standing in front of me with no plans to go anywhere or do anything, I will be your girlfriend again."

"Does that mean you are going to give Tyler another blow job?"

"Maybe," Erica replied.

"F-U-C-K!" I yelled. "You drive me nuts!"

"You're lucky I am in love with you. That is all I can say about all this," Erica said.

"What do you mean by that?" I asked.

"Oliver, I need to go now, bye..."

"Wait," I said.

"What?"

"I love you."

"I love you, too."

After this conversation, I had a lot to think about. Erica knew exactly how much pain it would cause me to hear that she was fooling around with Tyler. Now, I understood how she felt when she heard that I fooled around with Julie. The difference is that I just found out the hard way that she had the upper hand in our relationship, period.

Unfortunately, when I got off the phone with her, I still didn't understand the status of our relationship. I wanted to be 100% committed, but I couldn't come back to Ogallala if I planned to accomplish my goals. The irony was that Erica wouldn't commit to a relationship if I didn't go back home. However, if I went back home without figuring out how to pay for a heart transplant, Erica's father would die. I wanted to go home so bad that it drove me crazy, but this was not the noble road to follow. I could only provide happiness that comes from romantic love. Happiness that comes from fatherly love I couldn't personally provide, nor could her father if he was dead. Erica needed her father's love as much or more than she needed mine. That's why I didn't leave for Ogallala the moment our conversation ended.

Chapter V

THE FOLLOWING MORNING, I took a taxicab to the Greyhound bus station and bought a ticket to Seattle. There wasn't any particularly good reason to go to Seattle except that it was relatively close to Portland, and I could travel to this destination in less than a day. I pondered some interesting details about my future while on this bus ride. I thought hard about returning to my hometown in the near future to embrace Erica's love, but my mind had more than my heart's desire to ponder. It also had to settle a debate with my conscience, a horny teenage libido, my two goals in life, and the haunting image of Erica giving Tyler a blowjob. This wasn't an easy decision, nor was it completely decided on that bus ride.

Fortunately, these thoughts faded into the Seattle skyline shortly after arriving at the bus station. Seattle is a big city, but it felt completely different from southern California. Maybe it was truly unique, or maybe I just felt good about being there. All I know for sure is it was emotionally appealing and filled with scenic beauty. I remembered walking down to the pier after leaving the bus station. A variety of boats and barges were in Puget Sound. This harbor was so close that I could reach down and feel the water right in front of me.

When I looked towards the north across the harbor, Mt. Vernon and Mt. Baker were hiding a little too far in the distance to see, but when I turned around looking out toward the southern horizon, I could see snow-capped Mt. Rainier towering over the world and everything around it. This wasn't just an ordinary mountain that I was looking at. Mt. Rainer is a legendary active volcano that could destroy everything around it for hundreds of miles if it exploded. Lucky for me and everyone in Seattle, Mt Rainer didn't erupt that day. This volcano just stood majestically in the distance, covered with snow. Without even turning my head, I saw a giant Ferris wheel near the pier and the Space Needle in the distance towering above the skyline of downtown Seattle.

I walked down the sidewalk adjacent to Puget Sound for several minutes until I found Pikes Place Fish Market. This was a fascinating place just a block away from the harbor. There were all sorts of fresh food stands everywhere I looked. The most exciting thing about this place, in my opinion, was the fresh fish stand. I stood there listening to the cashier yelling out the type of fish the customer ordered. Within seconds, a market employee would pick up a big slab of fish meat, or even an entire fish, and yell out, "Incoming." The fish would then be tossed ten feet across the market stand into the hands of another employee. This person would catch the fish with a big piece of white paper, quickly wrap it up, and set it on the counter in front of the customer before they even thought about how to pay for it. I'd never seen anything like it.

After spending most of the morning walking around this marketplace, I decided to start walking toward the Space Needle. This was an observation tower that reminded me of one in Las Vegas at the Strat Hotel & Casino. I sat in front of this building for a couple of hours, drawing and writing while trying to sell the ten new zines of poetry I had created. I was impressed and surprised to have sold all ten copies quickly within those hours of creativity. It was a fitting reward to spend these ten dollars on my entrance fee to visit the observation tower in the Space Needle. When I looked around Seattle from the top of the Space Needle, it was an incredible site to see and worth all the hard work it took to get here.

After taking the breathtaking view from the Space Needle, I didn't have a specific plan, so I walked back toward Puget Sound until I reached Elliot Avenue. I followed this road located one block away from the harbor, headed back north toward Pike Place Market, hoping to find something interesting along the way. It wasn't long before I stumbled upon an interesting street filled with young people riding skateboards, kicking around hacky sacks, and just looking cool.

There were also several people selling jewelry and trinkets of all sorts, which they had spread over the tops of blankets. Along with many other kids my age, and the general public passing through, I walked down the street admiring the many trinkets for sale. Eventually, I stopped to look at some jewelry being sold by a girl about my age with short, twisted dreadlocks tucked under a hippy hat. She was in the middle of making a necklace when I looked down at all the unique pieces of jewelry she made.

"See anything you like?" she asked.

"Everything looks really cool," I responded. "It's hard to decide."

"Thanks, cutie. Feel free to try one on if you find something you like."

"What do you think would look good on me?" I asked. "Bracelet or necklace?"

"Bracelet," she confidently responded.

"Okay, which one?"

"Mmm... when is your birthday?"

"September 28th."

"Your birthstone is sapphire," she said. "What's your favorite color?"

"Green."

"Hey, that's my favorite color," she replied. "Okay, a few more questions... what is the first letter of your name?"

"O."

"What's the last letter of your name?"

"R."

"What's the second letter of your name?"

"L."

"Okay, last question," Jasmine replied. "What's your name?"

"What in the world?" I responded. "If you were going to ask me my name, then why did you ask me about the letters?"

"Just cause," she answered, giggling.

"I thought for a second that you would predict my name."

"No, sweetheart... I don't read minds, and I don't tell fortunes. All I know is that different colors found in certain stones represent different months... and I have a lot of them."

"Do you have that stone that you were talking about?"

"Which stone... your birthstone?"

"Yeah, that one."

"Unfortunately, no," Jasmine said. "I'll tell you what I do have."

"What's that?" I asked.

"Hold out your hand and close your eyes."

"Okay," I replied, holding out my hand and closing my eyes as she instructed. Then, I felt a bracelet set on my hand.

"You can open your eyes now," Jasmine said. "I hope you like it."

Looking down at the bracelet she set in my hands, I felt like I had found what I was looking for. The bracelet was made of hemp and had three colorful glass beads that looked awesome. This may have been the perfect bracelet for me. "This is awesome!"

"I'm glad you like it," Jasmine said with a big smile. "You know that you still haven't told me your name."

"Oh, I'm sorry.... My name is Oliver."

"It's nice to meet you finally, Oliver," Jasmine replied. "What do you think about your bracelet?"

"It's perfect," I replied, 'How much does it cost?"

"Mmmm... ten dollars?"

"That sounds like a fair deal to me," I replied, reaching into my pocket for money. "This made my day."

"What are your plans for this evening?" Jasmine asked.

"I have no idea," I responded. "I just got here."

"You look a little lost," Jasmine said. "Are you from around here or are you just a tourist who likes to look at hippy jewelry?"

"No," I answered, intrigued that she described her craft as hippy jewelry because that is precisely how I would have described it. "I traveled here from Nebraska, and I don't have any friends here. Honestly, I don't know what I will be doing this evening. Eventually, I will need to find a place to sleep. Are you from Seattle?"

"I moved to Seattle from South Bend a few weeks ago," Jasmine replied. "I haven't made any friends yet, either. The only people I have met are my roommates and some of their friends."

"Aren't you friends with your roommates?" I asked.

"I guess so, ya, but I just met them," Jasmine replied. "I'm renting a room out of a six-bedroom house about four blocks away, but I can't live there for much longer."

"Why is that?" I asked.

"If you met them, you would know why. They are nice guys, and I get along with them, but they are total slobs. All they do is party all night and sleep all day. If they aren't partying or sleeping, all they do is play video games and practice their music."

"How do they manage to pay rent?"

"That is the one thing that is pretty cool about living with these guys," Jasmine explained. "They happen to be band members of Embassy."

"Embassy, never heard of them."

"They are the best punk rock band on the West Coast. They just got back from touring southern California. They sold out the Roxy Theater, the Troubadour, and Whiskey a Go Go in West Hollywood during a three-day punk rock festival in West Hollywood, and they played in San Bernardino at the Orange Pavilion. They were the opening band for Green Day and Blink 182. Do you listen to punk rock? Wait a second... I forgot that you are from Nebraska," she said, starting to giggle. "You probably listen to country music or something, huh?"

"You would think that, wouldn't you?" I said, smiling. "I listen to all sorts of music, but I do listen to a lot of punk rock music!"

"You have to check out Embassy! They are putting on a show tomorrow night," Jasmin said. "Do you want to go?"

"Sure... that sounds awesome!" I said. "I have nothing better to do. What is your number? Maybe I could just give you a call tomorrow before the show?"

"If you have no friends here and have no place to stay, then why don't you just stay the night at my house?" Jasmine said with a seductive smile.

"Really?" I asked, trying to understand the mystery of being hit on by this gorgeous hippy chick.

"Yeah, really... people are always crashing out at our house. Nobody will mind."

"Okay... thank you so much! That's really nice of you," I replied, feeling more grateful to have a new friend to talk to than having a place to stay that night.

Chapter VI

Jasmine seemed to be a very cool girl. We talked into the late afternoon. I couldn't help but notice how physically fit she was. It looked like she spent a lot of time in the gym, but I didn't figure she did. She also had big breasts. It was hard not to look at this woman. I wasn't the only man noticing this. Nearly every guy that passed by took a wandering gaze in her direction. She knew this about herself and would mindfully move around in seductive ways as potential male customers walked by. I wasn't paying much attention, but a few times, she'd get up and bend over at the waist to pick up a piece of jewelry. She made it impossible for her male customers to avoid a solid gander.

There were a few people here and there who would stop to look at her jewelry. I noticed that she sold one necklace to a woman in her mid-thirties. She sold a few other types of jewelry and trinkets to an assortment of men walking by as well, but business seemed a little slow. However, as people crowded the streets during rush hour, she began to sell several more pieces. At one point, I noticed a group of ten men or more who seemed very interested in her hippy jewelry. I was impressed that her craft attracted so much attention. I was surprised to see that hippy jewelry was so popular with the office crowd. I was even more surprised to see her sell several pieces of jewelry made of glass beads and hemp to guys wearing suits. She sold over a dozen pieces of jewelry in less than an hour.

At one point, I stood up to work out the pins and needles I felt in my feet from sitting on the hard cement for so long. As I looked down at Jasmine wheeling and dealing with a well-practiced sales pitch to several young men, realized a legitimate reason for her peculiar success. Her top was hand-made from corduroy. It was a loose-fitting garment that was about eight to ten inches in length, and it went all around her breasts and back like a barrel. It hung over her shoulder with two small strings. When she was sitting down facing directly toward me, it completely covered her breasts, but when she bent over, the men were seeing more than if she was wearing a bikini top... much more. Her top hung down, allowing men passing by to take a magnificent gander at her bare, naked, well-developed teenage breasts. I was standing in a crowd of men when I noticed this. I wasn't trying to be a pervert or anything, but her naked breasts were jiggling, and she must have had an ice pack hidden in her top somewhere because her quarter-sized nipples were rock hard. I already purchased one bracelet, but this nearly convinced me to buy a few more.

Sometime near sunset, she had a rather dorky, overweight man dressed in a suit that looked like it was purchased at Alan David Custom Suits on Fifth Ave in New York City. He looked ready to buy Jasmine's most expensive piece of jewelry. "Here, sit down for a minute on this pillow," she told her overly excited male customer. "I'll give you a palm reading while you decide on which piece of jewelry you plan to buy from me." After the man had sat down, she set some pieces of her most expensive jewelry between her legs. Then, she adjusted her dress, pulling the garment well passed her knees while spreading her legs, and then she pretended to observe the palm of his hand. Then, she started to move around the piece of jewelry. "Look closely," she said. "See how the beads still sparkle even if I move them under the shade of my dress?"

The man nodded in response to her promiscuous sales pitch, "Feel free to stare as long as you like. The great thing about this piece of jewelry is it can get wet. Okay, one more thing I want to show you. If I move this piece of jewelry out into the sun like this...it costs twenty dollars, but if I move it out of the sun way up here right next to my..." Jasmine leaned in and put her hand to the side of her mouth as if to hide her words, "Pussy, the price goes up to forty dollars. Let me look at your palm one more time. Yep, it says that is the one you want. Are you ready to close on this deal?" Jasmine said to this man, who was now nearly drooling. He nodded in total agreement to whatever Jasmine was saying to him.

When he took out his wallet, Jasmine and I watched as he thumbed through several crisp hundred-dollar bills, searching for smaller increments. "Wait, hold on a second," Jasmine said, grabbing the man's wrist. "Actually, I am prepared to offer you a deal of a lifetime. I need to whisper this into your ears because I can't be advertising this deal to just anyone."

I saw this perverted man smile while he quickly took out a hundred-dollar bill from his wallet. After Jasmin tucked the bill away, I saw her guide the perverted man's hand under her dress. "One Mississippi, two Mississippi, three Mississippi, four Mississippi, and five Mississippi... ok, buddy, you're done," Jasmine said, immediately standing up.

"Oliver, you didn't see that, did you?" Jasmine, asked after the man walked away.

"See what?" I asked.

"Exactly!"

It took only a minute or two for Jasmine to pack up her makeshift store. She put all her jewelry into a large bag that she could easily carry over her shoulder. Before we walked away from this makeshift hippy market, Jasmine took the money out to count. I figured the wad of cash she counted to be over three hundred dollars. It looks like you have a lucrative business," I said, not really thinking through my words before I said them.

"Are you judging me?" Jasmine quickly snapped back.

"No," I promptly replied. "I really didn't mean it like that."

"Mean it like what?" she asked.

"Shit. I'm sorry," I said. "I'm just going to stop talking now."

"Oliver, you are fine," Jasmine said, as a big, gorgeous smile returned to her pretty face. "My store is typically a look but don't touch operation. You just saw a very rare exception. A hundred dollars in five seconds… that is hard to pass up. I don't care who you are. Here is the thing, Oliver. I can sit out here working away making jewelry and only come up with maybe fifty or sixty dollars on a good day, but if I show off my tits and give an occasional pussy flash, I can make as much as four hundred dollars in a day. Some strippers don't even make that much, and they dance around a greasy pole in a sleazy nightclub while perverted guys stuff one-dollar bills into their G-strings."

"I don't have any opinions on this," I answered. "I want you to know that."

"Yeah, I'm sure you don't."

Within a few minutes, we were already at her house. When we entered the front door, two guys were on the couch playing video games. "Hey, guys, this is a friend of mine, Oliver. He is going to stay here for the night and go to your show tomorrow."

"Hey Oliver, I'm Ben."

"Nice to meet you," I said.

"Do you want a beer?" Ben asked.

"Yeah, I wouldn't mind one. Thanks!"

"Grab one for me, too," Jasmine said.

"Right on. I just bought a case of Schlitz and ten 40-oz Mikeys. Which would you prefer?" Ben asked.

"Mmmm.... that is a hard decision, the cheapest of all beers or the shittiest kind of malt liquor. Let's go with the Schlitz."

We sat on the couch for several minutes before the other guy introduced himself. Finally, he paused his video game, opened his beer, and said to me, while looking out of the corner of his eye, "I'm Cassidy. What's up?"

After watching Cassidy and Ben play video games for a little while, Jasmine got up to grab us a couple more beers and then asked me if I wanted to go upstairs to her room to listen to music. After the door was shut behind her, we sat on her bed, "If my roommates ask, tell them that we were friends growing up or something."

"Why?" I asked.

"I just don't want them to think I just met you and invited you to stay the night. It's the old double standard. If a man has a one-night stand, he is a stud. If a woman has a one-night stand, she is a slut. They already know my morals are compromised while my store is open, and I don't want to hear about it. Besides that, Craig, who plays drums for the band, has a crush on me. Even though

I don't like him like that, it would make him pretty jealous if he thought that... well, you know..."

"Yeah, I understand," I said, feeling pretty much the same way about the situation as she did. We continued to enjoy each other's company and conversation for another twenty minutes, and then Jasmine asked me if I wanted another beer, which I agreed to.

"Wait here," Jasmine said. "I'll be right back."

I looked around her room while she ran down the stairs. Her room was pretty interesting because of the flyers and pictures of the shows she had hanging up. I figured she must have been going to shows since she was twelve to have seen this much shit. I also noticed that aside from a dresser, she only had an acoustic guitar in her room. I was happy to see her walk back with a glass bong and a couple more beers.

"What do you want to talk about?" Jasmine asked, after smoking nearly an entire bowl.

"I don't know... anything."

"Sex, drugs, rock and roll?" she responded while giggling. "No, really, tell me what it was like growing up in Nebraska."

"It was boring as hell," I responded. "The only thing fun to do there is fish and hunt."

"Eww," Jasmine responded.

"Why eww? Going fishing and hunting is awesome!"

"I am a vegetarian and would never even think about killing anything."

"I would," I replied. "Deer, pheasants, and walleyes are delicious!"

"Each to their own, I guess."

"How about you?" I asked. "What was it like in South Bend?"

"Like when?" she asked. "Like when I was kid, or like recently?"

"I guess both," I answered.

"My childhood sucked! I have no idea who my parents are. I lived with my uncle till I was fifteen, be he raped me and went to prison. After that, I lived with my second cousin until I graduated from high school. All I have to show from my childhood is anxiety, trust issues, and a mild case of daddy issues."

"Holy shit, that's pretty heavy to hear," I responded, not coming up with a solid segue toward a better conversation. Nevertheless, after some awkward silence, I tried my best to move the conversation in a different direction. "Any recent experiences worth talking about... maybe something not trauma related?"

"I don't know... I guess people thought that my friends and I were a little strange because we spiked our hair and dyed it crazy colors, and then I began to grow dreadlocks my senior year. My boyfriend skateboarded instead of playing high school sports, so some people would call us potheads and think we worshipped the devil. Other people thought that we were gay. It wasn't because we were any of those things. It was just because we were a little different."

"I understand," I replied. "I'm not exactly normal, either."

"After I graduated from high school, I broke up with my boyfriend and followed Phish for about a year, so I did a lot of drugs and went to a lot of concerts."

"Really?" I responded. "Were you at the three-day show at the Gorge Amphitheatre earlier this summer?"

"Hell yeah, I was there! That was one of the most bitchin' times of my life!" Jasmine responded. "Why were you there, too?"

"Yeah, I drove up from southern California with my friend Fredrick, who had a boatload of acid to sell. Then, you know that orange Pinto with that giant bag of mushrooms?"

"Hell yeah, I do," she replied. "The one with the sign sticking out of it with a ten-dollar price tag?"

"Yep, that's the one!"

"Yeah, I remember that bag of mushrooms and that Pinto quite fondly, actually. I sold my jewelry and grilled cheese sandwiches a few lots down from that guy."

"Wow! I can't believe that we were that close to each other," I said. "Anyway, we took that bag back to southern California with us."

"Small world," Jasmine said. "What did you say your friend's name was again?"

"Fredrick," I said. "He's a great guy. He makes glass pipes and sells an ass load of drugs... super nice person."

"Is he tall with dreadlock's going down half his back and drives a moron van with tie-die curtains by chance?" Jasmine asked.

"Yes," I replied, "Do you know him or something?"

"Yep, I sure do. Everyone on the Phish tour knows him. He's a goddamned legend!"

"Really?" I asked. "Like how?"

"For a few reasons, actually... for one, he always has the best LSD on the tour, hands down... and have you ever noticed how much acid that guy eats?" Jasmine asked wide-eyed.

"Yeah, it's pretty nuts," I said.

"If you came to the Phish show with him, then I'm sure you know what else he's good at," Jasmine said with a smile and rolling eyes.

"Yeah, he is good at blowing glass," I said.

"Oh, he is good at more than blowing glass."

"What do you mean?"

"Come on… didn't you see all the women standing around his van after the shows?"

"Yeah… now that you mention it."

"All us girls call him Magic Tongue… if pussy licking was an Olympic sport, that boy would be on the cover of a Wheaties box."

"Really… Fredrick?"

"Ooooooohhh… yes… Mr. Magic Tongue Fredrick."

"Wow, I never would have guessed."

"The more you know…. Well, I'm pretty tired, how about you?"

"Yeah, I'm getting sleepy too," I said, as Jasmine stood up from her bed and slipped her loose-fitting top right up over her head. Then, her hippy dress effortlessly fell to the floor. I didn't know what to do, but I couldn't look away because she was like a Playboy model. Jasmine stood naked in front of me for a few seconds before she turned off all the lights in her bedroom except for a desk lamp. Then, she walked back over to the bed and stood in front of me again, now staring into my eyes.

"What are you waiting for?" Jasmine asked.

"Waiting for what?" I asked.

"Stand up."

"Okay," I said, and as I did, she kneeled down in front of me and aggressively pulled my pants to my ankles. She sucked my cock for several minutes, and this wasn't just to pleasure me. After nearly bringing me to an orgasm, she stood back up to make out with me while jerking me off. This was the first opportunity I had to actually feel Jasmine's breasts, which were a perfect amount of squishy for the world's best titty fuck. Looking at me unsuspectingly with big brown eyes and a seductive grin, I spent the next several minutes thoroughly licking every place a woman felt pleasure. As this sexual dance became more aggressive, she reached over to turn up the music really loud.

"Why do you want the music so loud?" I asked.

"I don't want my roommates to hear my ass clap."

Chapter VII

I WOKE UP FROM a restful night of sleep. As I opened my eyes, I was suddenly hit with the blunt edge of an unpolished memory. A pretty face and naked body left me with another reason to believe that every girl was secretly wild and erotic. I was lying face to face with Jasmine when she opened her eyes. "Good morning, psycho," Jasmine said, in a very quiet voice. "Do you always watch people sleep?"

"I just think that you are pretty."

"That's sweet of you," she replied, as she reached down and grabbed my cock. I became instantly hard with new guilty pleasures as Jasmine turned to her side. She then gently moved her ass back and forth with a sleepy desire to have sex again. A few seductive moments would pause time briefly before Jasmine asked, "Oliver?"

"Yes," I answered unsuspectingly.

"When are you going to start doing naughty things to my ass?" This wasn't so much a question as it was a command. The mystery of women would not be solved this particular morning. Jasmine made me feel guilty, innocent, misery, pleasure, sad, happy, anxious, and inner peace all at the same time. We lay in bed until the afternoon came.

When we walked downstairs to eat a late breakfast, Jasmine apparently had zero fucks left to give. It was only yesterday she confessed a desire to keep one of her roommates' sexual desires at bay. She was wearing around my tee-shirt like a trophy, and only my tee-shirt, which seemed to cover a little over half her ass.

We were eating breakfast, smoking bowls, and drinking coffee in the dining room. She would sit and cross her legs as men would come, then uncross them and bend over as much as possible a they would go. She wanted to prove beyond a shadow of a doubt that I had gotten lucky, while she intentionally filled the rest of the house with jealousy. At one point, she pulled my shirt down in an insufficient attempt to cover herself. Then, she ran into the living room where all her roommates were sitting watching TV to ask what only appeared to be an important question. A short time later, Jasmine finally decided to put on pants.

After we showered and got ready for the day, Jasmine asked if I wanted to come down to the market with her for a few hours. I agreed because I had absolutely nothing better to do. On this day, Jasmine wore a completely different clothing ensemble. I was not surprised that it was also carefully prepared to allow for exhibition at her discretion.

This was a Saturday, so a much different crowd was passing by. On Friday afternoon, the crowd was more of a business class of people who had finished working for the day. Many were walking to happy hour, and others were heading home to their families. Today, there were substantially more tourists and weekend warriors out for a stroll. I noticed that caused Jasmine to adjust her sales tactics because she made nearly all of her sales without any fleshy persuasion like she had been doing the day before.

While Jasmin was wheeling and dealing with her jewelry, I saw that a Kinkos copy center was just down the street, so I decided to walk over and get ten more copies of <u>My Writes</u> zine printed off. When I returned, I set them on Jasmine's blanket and attempted to passively sell them to the people who stopped to look at Jasmine's jewelry. Most of my afternoon was spent finishing up a drawing I had been working on. This was really colorful artwork, and I thought it was one of the most unique pictures I ever created. By the time I finished this picture, I noticed only one more copy of <u>My Writes</u> left on Jasmine's blanket. Just before Jasmine began to gather up her jewelry to go home for the day, I returned to Kinkos to print ten more copies. Our plans at this point were liquid and only included seeing her roommate's band play at a concert that night.

Jasmine's roommates were packing their van with their equipment and preparing to set up for their show when we returned to Jasmine's house. One of the guys I had not met yet gave me a strange look. Ben and Cassidy were cool and didn't think too much about me returning to their house with Jasmine. As we approached the van, a conversation started, and I was introduced to the remaining band members.

"Hey guys, what's up?"

"How's it going ... Oliver, right?" Ben asked, holding out his knuckles for a fist bump.

"You got it," I replied. "Are you guys getting ready for the show tonight?"

"Yeah, the show starts at nine," Ben replied. "Are you coming to the show?"

"Hell yeah!" I replied. "Sounds like it's going to be awesome."

"Right on," Ben replied.

The guy who gave me a strange look the night before made it a point to shake my hand. "My name is Paul."

"Oh, I'm sorry," Jasmine interrupted, "Everyone, this is Oliver." She then pointed out the other two remaining band members, "That's Hugh, and that's Blain."

"What's up, guys! Awesome to finally meet you," I responded. "Jasmine has told me a lot about Embassy. Jasmine says your band rocks hard!"

"Yeah, well, Jasmine usually gets pretty drunk at all our shows, so I don't know how much I would trust her opinion," Blain said.

"Whatever, Blain," Jasmine responded.

"What instruments do you all play?" I asked out of curiosity.

"I play the sax. Blain plays the harmonica. Hugh plays the bagpipes. Ben plays the banjo, and dipshit here, plays with himself mostly," Cassidy sarcastically responded while pointing at Paul. "Na... just kidding, man. I'm the lead singer and play rhythm. Blain is bass and backup vocals. Ben is lead guitar. Hugh sings a few songs and plays whatever instrument he feels like playing, and Paul plays with himself like I said the first time." The guys were all laughing at Cassidy's joke. I could tell that Paul caught a fair amount of shit from these guys.

"Hey, fuck you," Paul said, as he pointed his middle finger at Cassidy.

"What instrument do you play?" I asked.

"I play drums," Paul replied. "Cassidy is just an asshole."

We arrived at the show at about seven that evening, which was a full hour before the first band was scheduled to start playing. There were two things that I totally wasn't expecting when we showed up at the concert. The first thing was that it was an outdoor venue with a big stage set up in a park adjacent to Puget Sound. I was expecting this show to be in a dingy theater somewhere like the punk rock concert I went to in Portland. The second thing that I wasn't expecting was that there was already a giant crowd of people when we got there. Since we arrived an hour early, I figured that it would only be me, Jasmine, and some band members standing around.

Jasmine and I got into the concert with a couple of guest passes that Embassy gave her. As we began to walk around the crowd, Jasmine seemed to know an awful lot of people. This surprised me because she told me that she didn't have many friends in Seattle. At one point she told me to wait by the stage as she went off by herself to mingle. Then she came back about twenty minutes later with a large bottle of Yukon Jack 100-proof whisky and offered me a couple of swigs. I didn't know what I was getting into with this stuff. After only two shots, I already felt a buzz, and it left such a foul taste in my mouth it nearly caused me to hurl.

It wasn't long after this that the first band started to play. According to the flyer, three bands were going to play that night. Embassy was the headliner, so I figured they would be the last. The music played by the opening band didn't impress me much, but it was such an incredible venue that I was barely paying attention to the music. The sun was setting over the water during the first set, and it was absolutely gorgeous.

About twenty minutes into the first set, Jasmine asked me to follow her backstage, where we met up with the entourage rolling with Embassy and the second band scheduled to play that night, Two Minutes Hate. Everyone was hanging out on a bunch of old couches and drinking from a keg that sat right behind the stage. Shortly after Jasmine and I sat down on one of these couches, Cassidy approached us with a joint and offered to get us a few beers from the keg. About ten minutes after these beers were handed to us, I noticed that Jasmine was sipping rather heavily on her bottle of whiskey and seemed to be using her beer only as a chaser.

We sat backstage through the rest of the first band's set and then tried to work our way to the front of the stage when Two Minutes Hate were getting ready to play. This band was really good, but their set wasn't nearly as long as I was expecting it to be. It only consisted of six or seven songs, and they didn't say much in between songs. I was really enjoying their music and wished they had played longer.

By the end of this set, I noticed that Jasmine was getting pretty trashed, which severely altered her personality, and showed off a character that I didn't really care to know. Until now, I had thought that Jasmine had a somewhat passive personality besides her low-key exhibitionism, but the booze made her loud and obnoxious. I learned this more during the last set change when she took me by the hand and led us around the crowd to meet all her friends whom she had described not having only a day earlier.

I felt saddened seeing her slobber over everyone we ran into as we made our way through the crowd and back toward the front of the stage. Maybe I was being a little jealous, or perhaps, my own buzz was swaying my judgment, but it bothered me. After we had finally made our way to the front of the stage, she began to hang all over every guy that walked passed her. I noticed that some guys avoided her because of this, and others tried to take advantage of her drunken personality. I had only drank a few beers when I witnessed her personality change. This was an experience that would help me address my own issues with alcohol some years later, but for now, it just made me feel shitty.

I didn't think much more about this once Embassy got on stage. When they started tuning their instruments, the atmosphere changed completely. The crowd started cheering like crazy when they heard the sounds of their instruments being tuned. I thought to myself that if the crowd was going this nuts over Embassy tuning their instruments, they were going to go absolutely bonkers when they actually started playing music, and I was right.

Everyone in the venue began pushing and shoving their way to the front with wild anticipation just before the first song was played. Moments later, three or four hundred people created one of the biggest mosh pits I have ever seen in my life, and I've been to a lot of punk rock concerts over the years, including a couple of warp tours. As soon as Embassy began to play, I understood why so many people liked them. Each band member was incredibly talented and displayed a deep passion for music. One of the things I was most impressed by was that I could actually understand the lyrics of these songs because the lead singer's voice was rough and loud. Also, every band member, including the drummer, sang backup vocals throughout their set.

Embassy played a set that consisted of at least fifteen or more songs. I was amazed at their diversity of musical talent, and every one of their songs was unique and awesome. I was most impressed with the songs when Cassidy, Ben, and Hugh created harmony by playing three guitars simultaneously while Blain played bass. I felt something deep and powerful in their music that just made me feel good about myself and the people around me.

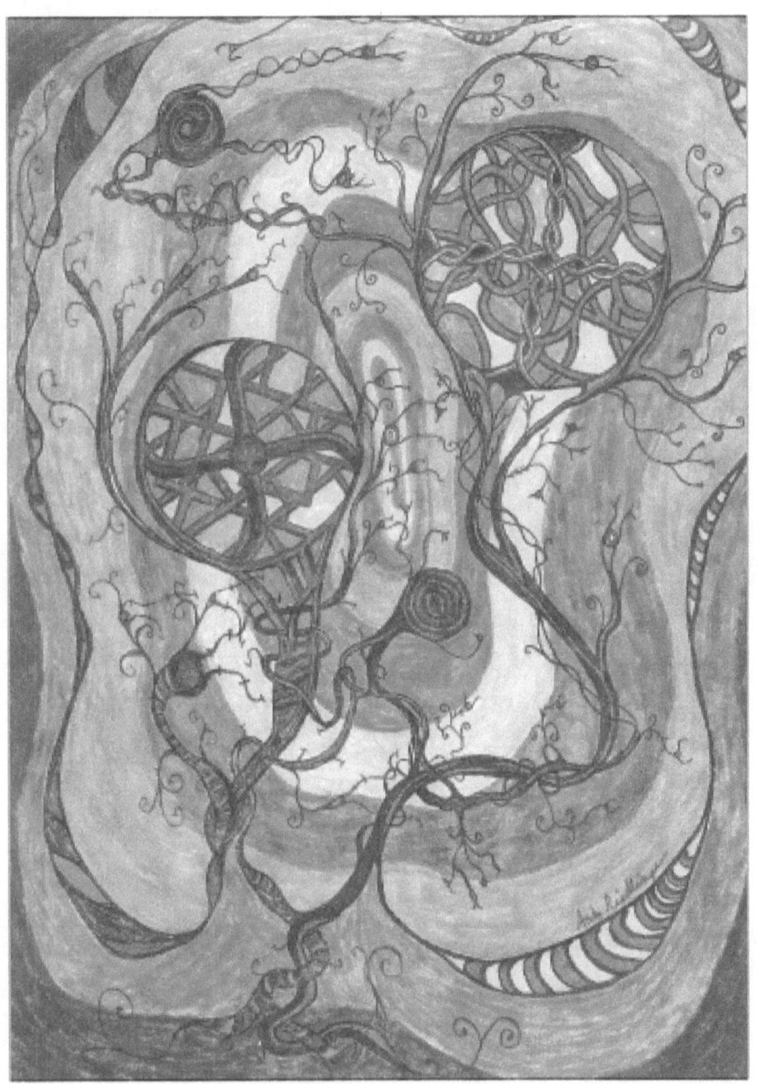

Picture drawn while Jasmine sold her jewelry.

Chapter VIII

When I walked passed the exit gate after Embassy's concert, everyone seemed to group together for several minutes with smiles on their faces. Cigarettes were being smoked, and sweat-soaked clothes were drying. At least for the moment, we all looked cool. Once all three bands finished loading their equipment into the back of their vans, we left for the after-party, which was unofficially organized back at Jasmine's house.

When we arrived, Ben and Blain were carrying a keg of beer, so I followed them to the backyard. Then, I watched as everyone stood around for a little while arguing about how to tap a keg. I thought it was a bit humorous listening to how they planned to get a better beer-to-foam ratio than the last party. Once the keg was tapped, a large crowd of people started flocking to get beer like a bunch of jocks at a high school homecoming party.

I stood in line to get a beer from this keg for an awful long time. This was probably because it wasn't a very organized line. More or less, it was just a bunch of kids standing around the keg, waiting for the next person to give them the tap. There were far more guys at this party than girls. This didn't surprise or bother me in any way. The only reason that I gave a shit at all about this ratio was because it seemed to screw up the rotation while I was waiting to get a beer.

Between the ladies and band members getting first dibs, I always seemed to be waiting at the back of the line.

After the band members filled their giant house mugs, they would always hand the tap to the prettiest girl they saw standing around the keg, and if that girl didn't give it to another girl, she would hand it back to the coolest, best looking guy she saw standing around the keg. Then, that guy would either hand it back to another girl or to one of his friends, which would only start another chain reaction that screwed up the rotation all over again.

Finally, one kid must have had pity for me. Despite everyone grabbing for the tap, claiming it was their turn, he handed me the tap and told everyone, "This kid has been in line forever."

"Thanks. I have been waiting so long that I wasn't sure if I'd get a beer before the keg ran dry," I responded. "I may as well just get back in line after filling this up."

"Yeah, I saw you waiting in line since I got my last beer, so I figured it was probably your turn," the decent human being said. "What's your name?"

"Oliver."

"My name is Bob."

"Good to meet you," I replied, extending my hand for a gentleman's handshake.

"How did you like the show?" Bob asked.

"The show was great," I replied, "but this party could be better. They need to get another keg or something."

"Yeah, they definitely need another keg," Bob replied. "I wonder if they have one?"

"I don't think they do," I replied.

"That sucks, but a keg isn't all this party needs," Bob replied, as he looked around the yard. "It needs some crazy ass shit to happen. Nobody is falling over yet. Nobody has gotten into a fight. I've only seen one person puke. This party needs something weird to happen soon, or it's not going to meet the usual standards for an Embassy after-party."

"Why do you say that?" I asked.

"Their parties are fucking nuts!" Bob replied. "Haven't you ever been to a party here before?"

"No, I'm just visiting," I answered. "I just came for the show."

"I thought Embassy's set rocked!"

"They are super talented!" I said.

"Yeah, they're unbelievable!" Bob commented. "Who are you visiting?"

"No one really," I replied. "I just met the girl that lives in this house, Jasmine."

"Are you in college?" Bob asked.

"No, I just graduated high school," I answered. "I'm just traveling around right now."

"By yourself?" Bob asked.

"Yeah, it's just me."

"Nice! Where have you been?"

"So far… just Las Vegas, Portland, and here," I replied, "but I'm planning to go down to San Francisco soon and eventually make my way down to southern California."

"That sounds like a great time," Bob replied. "I would be doing the same thing if I were your age."

"How old are you?" I asked out of curiosity because he didn't seem much older than I was.

"Twenty-four. I'm going to turn twenty-five next month."

"Really?"

"You seem surprised," Bob replied.

"I thought that you were a lot younger."

"I wish," Bob said. "I didn't think that I would ever grow up when I was eighteen. It didn't seem like I was getting older until I turned twenty. That's when I got my ex-girlfriend pregnant. I tried to keep going to school, but I couldn't afford college once my little one was born. I had to get a nine to five. I became an adult way too quick."

"Where did you get a job?" I asked.

"I install lighting fixtures in office buildings."

"That sounds like a cool job."

"Not as cool as a studio artist like I was going to school for," Bob replied. "I had a full-ride scholarship at Washington University. During my only year in college, I had an internship and got to meet the Wu-Tang Clan. I was the guy who pressed the record button when the Wu-Tang Clan recorded "For Heaven Sake" on their Wu-Tang Forever album. That's all I did was push one single button, but it changed my life because I got to hang out with Method Man, Ghostface Killah, U-God, and Cappadonna."

"You really met Method Man?" I asked, blown away by Bob's story.

"Fuck yeah! I met Method Man! The Wu-Tang Clan rented out the whole second level at the 700 Club that night! I wasn't even old enough to drink, but if you press the record button for one of their studio recordings, it doesn't make any difference. I sat down at a table with bottle service, and Method Man sat down right beside me. He smoked a blunt with me. Now, that was cool!"

"Why didn't you stay in school?" I asked. "That sounded like an awesome job! If you were in the studio with Wu-Tang Clan during your freshman year in college, I bet you would have met every badass rapper by now."

"I sometimes think about what my life would have been like if Joey wasn't born. All of a sudden, here I am with all sorts of responsibilities. I need to do adult things, like go grocery shopping and pay my ex-girlfriend child support, even though I watch Joey more than she does, that stupid bitch! But there isn't much that I can do about it. I tried to quit paying child support for a year, and I got put in prison for ninety days. So now, instead of thirty-three percent of my check going toward child support, forty-eight percent of my check gets taken out before my boss even hands me the envelope."

"What's child support?" I asked.

"It's when you lose a custody battle," Bob replied, pointing. "Who the hell is that?"

When I turned around, I saw Jasmine running toward me with her hand over her mouth, "Oliver, I am going to be sick," Jasmine said. Then, she puked all over a tree. There was puke everywhere. It didn't seem like there were many people at the party when I first started talking to Bob, but Jasmine's entire backyard was now packed shoulder-to-shoulder, and it seemed like everyone was suddenly looking at this tree. I felt so sorry for Jasmine when I looked down and saw her on the ground puking her guts out.

"Are you okay?" I asked.

"Leave me alone," Jasmine replied. "Can't you see I'm sick?"

"Do you need some water?" I asked while helping Jasmine stand back up. "Maybe some help getting up to your room?"

"I'm fine! I get sick at parties all the fucking time... I know what I'm doing," Jasmine replied. The last thing I heard her say as she began to stumble toward her house was, "What is with me?"

"It is starting to feel a little more like a normal Embassy after-party after all!" Bob said with a grin. "All we need now is for someone to fall down the stairs or get in a fight, and it will be right on track." Not long after he said this, things began to spiral out of control.

There weren't many places to sit at this party, so a bunch of drunk ass kids carried a couch from the front porch into the backyard and set it about thirty feet away from a barbeque grill. There was a tall guy with long brown hair that went down to his waist standing at the barbeque grill. I don't know where he found the charcoal, the spatula, or the lighter fluid. It was even a mystery where his burger came from. All I know is this guy was super stoked because he was about to eat the only piece of meat on the grill. He spent a solid hour cooking and preparing his burger until it was rendered to be nothing short of perfection. I remember him turning around after taking the first bite. He had a beer in one hand, a burger in the other, and a comb in his back pocket.

That guy was the happiest person at the party for sure! He was munching on his burger, grinning from ear to ear while he walked over to the sofa. However, I didn't notice this man's giant smile or the couple of extra bites missing from his burger because I was too busy watching some dumbass pour lighter fluid on the sofa. As soon as the happy burger guy sat down, that old piece of crusty furniture went up in flames. Moments later, the whole backyard smelled like burnt hair. I saw three-foot-high flames shooting off the top of that man's head for about two seconds. That's all it took. This poor guy had probably been growing out his hair for years, and now it was all gone. Incidentally, the same dumbass that started the couch on fire in the first place ran over and splashed beer all over his head to extinguish the flames. That is when the fight started.

As soon as the unsuspecting victim of these drunken shenanigans realized what happened, he stood up with a crazy look on his face. When I looked at him, he was still holding his burger and had smoke rising off his head. The dumbass that started his hair on fire was standing beside the couch laughing, but this wasn't funny at all. I was still trying to figure out where this resourceful person found the charcoal, spatula, and lighter fluid. Now I was trying to figure out where the hell he found the shovel he was waving around, "I'M GOING TO FUCKING KILL YOU!"

For the next several minutes, I watched a drunken idiot get chased around the party by a man with a shovel and no hair. This was when people realized there was a real possibility of this situation resulting in serious injuries, but with this guy waving a shovel around, nobody could do anything about it. To make a terrible situation even worse, the steel spade of this shovel somehow flew off while he was waving it around. When the steel spade hit the fence, the wooden handle hit the guy holding the shovel square in the face. Then, he started hobbling around, screaming, "Fuck! Fuck! Fuck! That fucking hurt!"

While everyone stood there watching this guy holding his face in utter agony, some girl with unexplained evil intentions pushed the poor bastard into the flaming couch headfirst. It's a good thing this guy didn't have any hair at this point because that would have been a disaster! Lucky for him, only his shirt caught on fire. As if this guy hadn't suffered enough, he now started to run around, trying to put out the flames shooting off his back. It took a while, but he managed to put out the fire. Unfortunately, as soon as the flames were extinguished, that same girl kicked him in the nuts so hard he dropped to his knees. I don't understand what got this girl so pissed off, but she began to whale on this guy for at least a minute or so before somebody finally decided to pull her off of him.

After this, I started to stand in line for the keg again. When I finally got to the end of the line and filled my beer, the guy with no hair came stumbling over to fill his cup. In addition to the third-degree burns on his head, he had bruises all over his face, and his shirt was burnt to crisp, but he still had an awesome beard. Everyone was so impressed that he lived through all this that they hoisted him up by his feet for a three-minute keg stand. The only reason they set him down was because the keg finally ran out.

It was past midnight at this point, but there were still an awful lot of people at the party, and it seemed like it was only getting bigger. I stood around with the guy with no hair admiring how oddly civil this party had gotten after this episode of total mayhem. I had figured the party would be over shortly after the flames were extinguished and the beer ran out, but I was wrong. When I went inside, I realized this party was nowhere near over. There was now a wide variety of cheap hard liquor sitting on the counter. That's when the people at the party started to get really drunk!

Occasionally, I went up to check on Jasmine because I felt that rape was in the air with so many assholes running around drunk as hell. I'd bring her a glass of water here and there, hoping she would feel better and maybe join the party again. I felt terrible that she was missing out on all the chaos. Unfortunately, she was way too drunk. I was all but certain that I wouldn't see her get out of bed till morning, but I was wrong about this, too. This night was full of surprises.

I'm not sure if it was bad luck, coincidence, or what, but despite Jasmine lying in her bed with her bedroom door closed, there were still two drunk men who wandered into her room that night. I was bringing up a third or fourth glass of water to Jasmine when I heard her screaming from the top of her lungs, "GET THE HELL OUT OF HERE, YOU SICK FUCKER!" A drunk man wandered into her bedroom and took a shit in her closet. All I saw was Jasmine pushing a naked man down the stairs and seeing turds flying every-where. Everyone at the party was so shocked when they saw this that nobody knew how to react.

However, after he tossed a turd into the living room, it was pretty obvious that he was going to get his ass kicked! The only reason the naked turd flinger is still alive is because of how fast he could run. All five band members from the Embassy ran out the door after him, but it was no use. I saw this naked man take off down the street faster than any drunk person I had ever seen run before.

There were a lot of people that left the party after the turd flinger ran away, so I easily found a place to sit on the couch in the living room. I must have passed out a short while later because the last thing I remember was the guy with no hair sitting on the couch next to me with a bottle of Jack Daniels. "Wanna shot?" he asked.

"Sure," I said, handing him my red plastic party cup. I was still holding my shot of Jack Daniels when I woke up an hour later. By this time, the guy with no hair was passed out next to me, and the only remaining people at the party were familiar faces I recognized from the concert. The drummer and lead singer from Two Minutes Hate, Cassidy, Ben, and Blain from Embassy, as well three slobbering drunk women were still partying their asses off.

Cassidy, Blain, and one of these three slobbering drunk women stood on the coffee table singing "Foolish Games" by Jewel. I found this surprising, but they sang every word in perfect harmony and sounded just like Jewel. After this 90's pop song was finished, they sang a song called "Nothing is Impossible" by a band called Fifteen.

You took your coat off. Stood in the rain. You're always crazy like that. And I watched from my window. Always felt I was outside looking in on you. You're always the mysterious one with dark eyes and careless hair. You were always crazy like that. Fashionably sensitive but too cool to care. You stood in my doorway with nothing to say. Besides some comment... on the weather. In case you failed to notice. In case you failed to see. This is my heart... Bleeding before you, this is me down on my knees. These Foolish games are tearing me apart. And your... Thoughtless words are breaking my heart.

Foolish Games, Pieces of You Album, Jewel 1995

Hey kid, I hope you know... sometimes life is going to suck! Hey kid, don't you know... sometimes everything is gonna be fucked up! Hey kid, don't you know... the only way around your problems is straight through them... Nothing is insurmountable... Nothing is un-doable... Nothing is unbeatable... Nothing is impossible.

Lucky, Lucky Album, Fifteen 1999

Nothing from this night was making any sense to me. As entertaining and strange as it was listening to these songs, I thought I better go check on Jasmine to see if she was doing okay. When I opened the door to her room, I saw some dude standing at the side of her bed with his pants at his ankles who appeared to be jacking off. I yanked him out of her room by his ankles and dragged him down the stairs. Cassidy and Ben looked over at this crying, half-naked pervert hitting his head on every step. "WHERE IS THE DUCT TAPE?"

A short while later, this naked guy's hands were taped behind his back, and his feet were taped together at the ankles. For the next couple of hours, everyone at the party took turns holding him coffin-style while smashing his head into the front door. He was crying and yelling, "Stop.. please stop.. it hurts!" Everyone there almost puked from laughing so hard because his head repeatedly hit the door while being told, "Dude, open the door! Hey, man, turn the doorknob! You dumb ass... why do you keep hitting your head on the door?" The drunk pervert kept yelling, "I can't... come on guys... just let me go...

Chapter IX

The next day, I woke up lying on the couch with a horrible headache. I remember the house smelling like stale cigarettes, fresh shit, spilled beer, and puke. It was absolutely disgusting! I was incredibly hungover, and this terrible smell just made me feel sick. I felt so horrible that I barely got off the couch that day. Finally, at about four in the afternoon, I called a cab to take me to the hardware store so I could buy a lock for Jasmine's door.

After installing a deadbolt, a chain lock, and a new door handle, Jasmine came downstairs and sat with me as we watched the <u>Back to the Future</u> Trilogy. While we watched these movies, Jasmine cooked some frozen pizza. After eating a few slices, I must have passed out again because I remember waking up the following morning before anyone else was awake in the house. I turned on the TV for a while, hoping to find something worth watching, but the five channels that got reception were pretty basic. I had to decide between watching Jerry Springer, Judge Judy, an infomercial, and a Spanish soap opera. Unfortunately, I quickly became bored watching this shit, so I decided to go outside for a little while. I was wanting to go for a walk, which would have been nice, except it was raining. About twenty minutes later, I went back inside and found Jasmine making some breakfast.

"Hey, Oliver, do you want some pancakes?" she asked.

"Yeah, that sounds good."

"What are you going to do today?"

"I don't know… what do you have planned?" I asked.

"Since it is raining, I really can't set up my store or sell any jewelry, so I will likely just sit around the house getting drunk."

"Okay," I replied, "I think this is the last night I plan to stay in Seattle."

"Why is that?" Jasmine asked.

"I have some business in southern California."

"Like what?"

"It's a long story… too long to explain," I replied.

"Bummer," Jasmine responded.

That night was very mellow, leaving me feeling sad. I think this was because I felt like I had made friends with Jasmine and some of the guys I had met over the past few days. Jasmine came with me to the bus station the following morning. She decided to wait with me until my bus to San Francisco arrived. It had been delayed by an hour due to heavy rain. We talked about all sorts of things during that hour. Our conversation wasn't about anything particularly meaningful, but it was worth every minute.

As the time approached for my departure, I couldn't help but notice Jasmine's alluring smile, which seemed to add an attractive accent to everything she said. Her eyes conveyed a captivating story without the need for words. As I gazed into her eyes, I pondered where our individual journeys in life would take us. It saddened me to realize that it was very unlikely we would ever meet again.

We sat in the Seattle Greyhound bus station, holding each other's hands for the last several minutes we spent together. It felt like our farewell gained momentum with each passing moment. The words we spoke while saying farewell were true, the thoughts we exchanged were genuine, and our feelings were mutual. Finally, the time came when my bus arrived. Jasmine and I kissed each other before she walked out of the bus station, holding our friendship close. This moment deserved a longer goodbye. As I stood in the rain a few minutes while waiting in line to get on the bus, I wondered if this was how Erica felt about Tyler.

The bus station in downtown Seattle was filthy on the outside and smelled funny on the inside. Oddly enough, it reminded me of the classrooms near the men's locker room in the basement at my old high school. The windows connected to the outside world were hazy yellow and cracked. The entire station appeared to be poorly financed and lacking custodians. I was stuck inside while sitting on an uncomfortable plastic chair with no padding.

I sat on a chair watching an arrivals and departure sign whose electronics were on the brink of failure. This sign informed me that I was about to experience a sixteen-hour bus ride. It was obvious that I was about to undoubtedly experience an unpleasant trip from Seattle to San Francisco. However, nothing could have prepared me for the epic horror I would experience once I boarded that bus.

Since I had no luggage except my carry-on backpack, I was one of the first people in line when it was finally time to board the bus. At first, I was happy that I would no longer stand in the rain. Before boarding this bus, I didn't think through a single thought about how to mitigate the circumstances that would cause this trip to become more unpleasant. My ignorance was bliss as I paid no particular attention to where I wanted to sit. Unfortunately, I learned that it matters where you sit during long-distance mass transit in flight, on trains, or on buses.

At this point in my life, I had only two experiences with long-distance mass transit. The first was when my family took a vacation to Florida to see Disney World and Busch Gardens. We drove to Denver and stayed with a friend my dad knew from high school. Then, he drove us to the airport in the morning, where we boarded a McDonnell Douglas DC-10 aircraft. I was so excited to experience my first plane ride. However, I began to get sick immediately after take-off and stayed sick until after we landed.

I'm not sure what I had for breakfast that morning, but it must have been bigger than the biggest meal of my entire life. Even if I had pushed my stomach way past its limit, my ten-year-old stomach should not have been capable of creating such a horrific mess. The amount of partially digested food that shot out of my mouth during this four-hour flight was uncanny.

The sheer volume of vomit offered no worldly explanation other than demonic possession. Eyewitness descriptions of events verify this evil experience. You know how on The Exorcist when that girl's head spins all the way around, completing a 360? That same thing happened to me, except I was projectile vomiting the whole time. By the time we touched down in Orlando, I had created one epic mess. My whole family was covered in vomit, except for my dad, who somehow mysteriously disappeared during this entire flight. There is a theory that he occupied one of the two shitters on this plane for all four hours. However, this information has never been substantiated, and my dad has refused to offer any explanation to this very day.

My only other experience with long-distance mass transit oc-curred a week earlier on a three-hour bus ride from Portland to Seat-tle. This was a rather pleasant experience for numerous reasons. First of all, I had been hitchhiking with low-key favorable experiences, but it was also frustrating at times because I was at the mercy of whoever agreed to give me a ride. I really didn't have much control over the decisions made while traveling from one place to another. I couldn't even choose my destination.

I found the bus ride from Portland to Seattle incredibly efficient and inexpensive. It cost me only fourteen dollars, and there were three departure times to choose from throughout the day. I think this to be the reason that created a lot of empty seats, at least on the bus that I boarded. The bus smelled good, and the bus driver was friendly. Most importantly, I went to the bathroom before I left Portland and didn't feel uncomfortable the entire bus ride.

Since that short journey was so pleasant, I just thought that the biggest problem I faced was the boredom I would experience on a sixteen-hour bus ride. I didn't forget how shitty my first and only other experience with long-distance mass transit was. However, I felt confident that I was not experiencing demonic possession when I boarded this bus, nor was I being followed by a poltergeist. Despite my confidence in all things worldly when I boarded this bus, it has since become debatable that a supernatural evil was not present on this particular bus ride.

The people who began to fill the bus all seemed to be as thrilled about this bus ride as I was. Only a couple of smiles eluded the consistency in the general bad mood of everyone who boarded this Greyhound bus. Unfortunately, I failed to consider the impact of the unsuspecting passengers who collectively sold out every seat. I was also unaware that the bus driver would make an announcement to sit down and buckle up and that we couldn't change seats for any reason. A variety of concerns that were never discussed made it so we could not change seats for the entire bus ride. For the first minute after the bus driver's announcement, this made no difference to me.

I would soon learn from this nightmare as it began to unfold that you always want to sit as close to the front of the bus as possible. You also want to get a window seat on long mass transit trips for three reasons. One reason is that you can look out the window, and another is that you have additional options to rest your head. However, the most crucial reason in this particular story would be that it limits your exposure to other passengers. If you sit next to the window, you can only see or talk to one person. If you sit in an aisle seat, you have all sorts of people to potentially deal with.

I really could have sat anywhere I wanted to. Nevertheless, I chose an aisle seat six rows from the back. This bus had fifty-two rows of seats and two seats on each side of the aisle. This meant that, including the handicapped spaces, this bus had a total of one hundred and twenty seats. I chose a seat in the aisle six rows up from the back. When I sat in this seat, I just figured with little calculation that I would have more legroom, would be able to stand up to stretch occasionally, and it would theoretically be more accessible to move about the bus.

What I didn't consider was that by sitting in this seat, I would have to wait for exactly one hundred people to get off the bus before I could. This didn't just affect my arrival. It affected everywhere we stopped, which consisted of two rest areas and one truck stop. This added roughly an hour of extra time I would spend on this bus compared to a front-row passenger, adding to my frustrations about returning to my seat.

Except for the epic buffet table in Las Vegas, my diet since I left Nebraska mainly consisted of dollar menu items at Taco Bell, Burger King, McDonald's, and gas station hotdogs. My steady diet of junk food, in addition to the copious amounts of beer that I had recently drank, created a random laxative with an element of surprise. This would lead to a uniquely terrifying bus ride experience I would never want to relive.

Now I'm not going to tell you if this bus ride and my poor decisions caused me to shit my pants or not. However, what I can tell you is that if I did shit my pants, I would have blended in much better with the people who would soon be sitting around me. I hoped a nice, friendly person, preferably an attractive young woman or a pleasant old lady, would sit beside me. Unfortunately, very few attractive women or pleasant old ladies boarded this bus, and I watched this wish of mine fade into the foul odors of many smelly people.

As passengers started to trickle in, I saw several people standing around the bus without luggage. Then, I noticed that many of these people had clothes that were all nasty. As these people seemed to be oddly organized by an official-looking person of sorts, I overheard someone talk about the state wars of homeless people. What I gathered was that cities such as Seattle would gather up their homeless people and put them on a bus to send them to another city for the simple fact that they didn't want to deal with them. The homeless population they targeted were the people who had an elevated appearance of permanent disabilities, profound drug problems, and severe mental health issues. The type of people that, if the state didn't find a way to greatly mitigate their underlying issues, then they stood no chance to transcend beyond a life of perpetual homelessness.

When about half of the bus was full, I looked behind me and noticed that not a single person was sitting behind me yet. That was when I saw the official-looking person get on the bus. After walking down the aisle, she ended up standing right beside me. I suddenly became very nervous about this person. I was pretty sure that she was a type of law enforcement officer.

The twenty homely people I saw through my window some minutes earlier came onto the bus, and all twenty of them filled the seats behind me. At this point, I still had no obligation to sit in my seat. The bus driver had not made his announcement yet. I was free to sit wherever I wanted to. I wanted to move, but I didn't want to look like the reason I was moving was because of these people. The ladder of these thoughts kept me from moving.

The collective odor from these people was not entirely realized just yet, but some wore clothes that had not been washed in weeks. Many of them wore pants soiled with dried piss and shit. I would have had difficulty believing that any of these people had bathed in the past several days. I tried hard to pretend that these people didn't have such deep-rooted problems, but this became exceedingly difficult once I began to smell their problems. Before I go on, I want to emphasize that I do not discriminate in general and have a tendency to be very understanding of humanitarian issues, so I certainly don't want people to think I'm being insensitive. However, there is no way to sugarcoat this situation. If it were just sad and disturbing, I likely wouldn't want to tell anyone about it, but this was also very bizarre. The behavior of the people on this bus is why this bus ride sticks out in the litany of memories I have from visiting the West Coast.

Someone sat across the aisle, one row up from me, who had such a dreadful weight problem that he occupied two seats, and he still didn't fit. Being a caring and curious person, I immediately felt sorry for him. This man's weight problem was slightly worse than the obese kid who died back in Ogallala, Nebraska. I had no idea if this person also broke bizarre eating records, or if he had his name in the Genius Book of World records, but the sweatpants he was wearing seemed like that could compete as the largest pair of sweatpants ever worn. His short yet massive arms and chubby little hands stuck out from an inspirational tank top, whose smiley face message told everyone to "Have a nice day." Unfortunately, no one who sat near this person would be able to have a nice day.

There was absolutely no way either one of his short, stubby arms could reach around his gigantic ass cheeks. The problems this caused for this poor soul left nothing to the imagination. There were obviously a lot of issues that this man faced daily that made it extremely difficult to keep clean. Some conclusions from this dreadful observation showed up in the terrible aroma that helped make everyone on that bus feel more like a prisoner than a passenger. Adding to a heightened level of irritation caused by the hideous stench from this morbidly obese man, there was also an annoying sound created by a continuous buzzing of flies. This group of flies appeared to follow him around, and their excitement reached a fever pitch where his sweatpants failed to cover his ass crack.

I had one guy and one girl in front of me. The man had dyed spiked hair and face piercings of all sorts. He wore tight leather pants with a Dead Kennedys concert t-shirt and giant black combat boots worn over his pants almost to his knees. The man was also covered in tattoos, including on his neck and face. This was during a time in history when seeing someone with neck and face tattoos was still an extremely obscure experience.

The woman wore a short black skirt with fishnet leggings and a pair of black, high-heeled shoes. Her top was a purposefully crafted tee shirt with rips and tears that crudely covered her large breasts. This tee shirt was mindfully worn in combination with a black bra that was carefully constructed to enhance this woman's cleavage. She had a bald head, and her face was heavily pierced with a large septum ring attracting peculiar attention to her nose. These two people had an odd, disgusting odor that was made up of patchouli oil, spilled beer, cigarette smoke, and sweaty armpits. It was painfully obvious that neither one of these two people had even thought of bathing in weeks.

During this bus ride, I watched their unusual behavior elevate into obnoxious yelling and borderline violent fights with each other. As they got further into their bag of drugs, the suspicious looks on their faces became paranoid and quiet. It was somewhere in between these two unique behaviors that they asked if I wanted to take some drinks off their bottle of Jack Daniels and do some lines of coke with them. I respectfully declined their generous offer. I had never done cocaine before, and this wasn't a drug I was interested in taking at this point in my life. The actions and manners of these two people would further encourage me not to experiment with powders. Oddly enough, even after calculating the extravagant appearance and behavior of these two people, they were still easily the most ordinary and least smelly people who sat near me.

There are five basic human senses: touch, sight, hearing, smell, and taste. The sensing organs associated with each sense send information to the brain to help us understand and perceive the world around us. Everyone on that bus at least had the sense of smell sending some horrible information to their brain that dreadful day. The diversity in life experience and their inimitable connection to the world would define their ability to empathize with the world's stinkiest people. This would create vastly different perceptions and opinions of the smelly individuals on this bus.

Some people would perceive this horrible smell as a reason to feel sorry for themselves and those who sat near these unique people and their awful stench. Others would likely perceive this appalling smell as a reason to feel sorry for their friends and family, assuming they had these people in their lives. Then, there would be some like me who had good reason to feel sorry for the people these terrifying smells were coming from.

You could visually see the collective odor from the people sitting around me rise up and move about the bus, causing an enigma of unbridled funk. Adults pinched their noses, children stuck their fingers in their nostrils, and people of all ages desperately tried to wave the dark mystery of these volatile odors away from them. Heads began to turn in every direction to identify where the marathon of foul smell had started. The bus driver likely pushed the gas pedal, trying to outrun the funk. I am sure he contemplated hitting the brakes to try to stop it. Certainly, he also turned his steering wheel to try to avoid it. Unfortunately, there was no way to prevent the horrendous odor protruding from these people. Silent screams of unified terror echoed throughout the bus, and if the bus had vocal cords, it would be yelling, "Why me?"

Chapter X

Approximately eight hours after I boarded the bus in San Francisco, I looked out the window while traveling on Interstate 6, about forty miles south of the Oregon border. Finally, we came to a fork in the road, and the bus driver pulled into a gigantic Phillip 66 truck stop at this crossroads. We stopped here so the bus could re-fuel. This was a unique place for us to stop for several reasons. Most notably, this giant truck stop was in a tiny town called Weed. I shit you not, there is actually a town called Weed. This small town sat at an elevation of 3425ft, and it is only ten miles west of Mount Shasta, whose summit elevation is 14,180ft. This created some breathtaking views, which may have been the only good experience of this entire bus ride.

Unless you packed a sandwich or snacks before leaving Seattle, this was the first opportunity you had to eat in at least eight hours, which pretty much meant that all one hundred and twenty people were incredibly hungry. It was a shit show mess, to say the least. I'm surprised that Greyhound didn't have a better plan for this situation, but I guess this was exactly the spot where we had to stop to get fuel.

The first twenty people sitting at the front of the bus were very fortunate for several reasons during this particular stop. They could all run into the attached diner and order food with the near certainty that they would at least be able to pick up their food to go before the bus left. The rest of us were left eating whatever we could find at the truck stop convenience store.

I was roughly the eightieth person to walk into this store. When I got inside, I looked around and saw everyone grabbing candy bars, chips, soda, microwave burritos, and basically anything edible. I felt extremely fortunate to get the last microwavable Chuckwagon sandwich. This is about the time that the morbidly obese man who was sitting next to me came into the convenience store crying for some reason.

I had no idea what he was crying about. Maybe it was because someone called him a fat ass or said something else really mean to him. There is also a possibility that it had something to do with a food order at the attached diner. Maybe one of his family members just died. I had no clue. I just saw that he was crying. This caused me to pay closer attention to him because I was curious about why he might be crying, and I felt kind of sorry for him.

Then, he starts wandering around the store, grabbing the twenty or so remaining candy bars and bags of sweets off the shelves. These were the ones that people don't usually think of buying, like Big Chunk or black licorice. The lack of variety of candy made him even more upset, and so now I visibly saw tears dripping from his pudgy facial features, which was understandable because no sane person likes black licorice. Next, he went down the chip aisle and was equally disappointed to find only two remaining bags of chips. One bag was pickle-flavored chips, and the other was ketchup. I had no idea these two flavors even existed before this depressing moment in time.

Eventually, he made his way to the front of the store, holding this odd variety of candy and chips in his arms like a baby. Then, he dumps it all at the front counter after telling the clerk he will be back to pay for it and needs to get more things. That was when I noticed him go around the corner to the hotdog dressing station to grab the remaining ketchup, mustard, mayo, and relish packets. Then, he starts looking around the store to see if anyone is looking at him, and that's when he looks over at me. I had been pretending to look at magazines since shortly after I saw this gigantic man enter the store, but really I was watching this person's strange behavior. We looked at each other, and neither one of us looked away for several creepy seconds.

Finally, this eerie moment ended when I watched him pick up the spoon he found in some tubs of salsa and other condiments that had been sitting out all day. Then, he starts eating whatever is in these tubs with the weird plastic spoon provided to the public. Once he finished that, he got in line, standing behind about fifteen people waiting to check out. This is when I see him eyeing these weird, fried Mexican burritos that looked like giant fried egg rolls but were significantly less appetizing. They were kept on a heating shelf with JoJos, slices of pizza, and chicken fingers that were already purchased and eaten.

For reasons that I completely understand, nobody wanted to eat these weird, fried Mexican burritos that kind of looked like big fried egg rolls. This fat dude was near the last person in a very long line who approached a giant checkout counter with several tills and truck stop employees. By this point, nearly one hundred people had already checked out. That should give you an indication of how unappetizing these things looked. Even the gross-looking hot dogs, like the shriveled-up ones, and the way undercooked ones were purchased, but not these goddamned things. Anyways, this guy was fucking stoked!

He calls over one of the several clerks working at the counter, who bags these things up, which makes him quit crying. He could have quit crying a few minutes back while eating whatever the hell was in those condiment tubs. I'm not sure, and I guess it doesn't really matter. The point that I am getting at is that this man is now ecstatic. He is happy as a drunk clown getting a blowjob from Madonna... back when she was in her twenties and gorgeous. That's when I figured he would stay the course and go up to pay for this crazy ensemble of obscure food items. However, this is when things got even weirder. From where I was standing, it appears that he asked the clerk about some uncooked hotdogs, which was substantiated when the clerk left, and came out from the back refrigerator with three big packages of raw hot dogs.

Finally, he got up to pay for all these disgusting food items. He has a bag of sixty raw hotdogs, two bags full of hotdog buns, and one bag of an odd assortment of gas station junk food. I stood over by the magazine rack, watching all this go down, and I couldn't believe my eyes. I was beginning to get frightened because I had to sit next to him for another eight hours if I planned on continuing onward to San Francisco. I nearly abandoned this plan right there and then. I had to think long and hard about just staying in that town called Weed and figuring out a new plan.

Meanwhile, absolute chaos was beginning to ensue outside the truck stop. The twenty homeless people sitting behind me started wandering around the parking lot, asking everyone for change. I saw one lady appear to proposition a truck driver to trade money for sex, and it looked as if the truck driver accepted her offer. About thirty people were standing around the entrance of the convenience store smoking cigarettes, joints, crack, and PCP. One guy got so whacked out on the dust he went running shirtless toward Mount Shasta and never returned.

Perhaps the weirdest thing was that the two punk rockers that were sitting in front of me had somehow acquired a boombox and were playing death metal. This music was not very loud because of the limitations of this small stereo, but it was enough to inspire a crowd of people to dance around like fucking idiots. This is while the punk rockers stood in the middle of all of them, head-banging and playing air guitar.

Suddenly, the bus driver interrupts this bizarre pandemonium by yelling, "Get back on the bus, you crazy circus act freaks!" I was surprised that his persistence, patience, and eccentric efforts miraculously paid off for the most part. As I watched this strange spectacle of dysfunctional people make their way back onto the bus, I suffered from a minor panic attack, knowing my turn was coming soon. As I boarded and began to walk back to my seat, I had no hope that this bus ride would get any better, and I was right.

Nearly everyone had just eaten a bunch of junk food at a truck stop, which resulted in about half the bus getting stomach aches, and the next restroom was four hours away. To make this situation even worse, I spent this entire time watching this colossal person sitting beside me eat one raw hot dog after another. He finally finished the last one only minutes before we arrived at the final rest area.

At this point, pretty much everyone on the bus needed to take a dump. Fortunately, these were the nicest, most pleasant rest stops

I have ever seen in my life. However, once this crowd of traveling degenerates wreaked havoc on the place, it was no longer nice or pleasant. This shitty situation left the bathrooms completely deprecated.

The men's and women's rest stops combined to provide only twelve toilets, and eight were in the women's restroom. As you can imagine, along with the junk food we ate, this caused some serious issues. Once again, the first twenty or so people near the front of the bus had a delightful experience compared to the rest of the people sitting behind them. I was one of these people who had to stand in one of the two lines that formed outside the women's and men's restrooms. These lines were as ridiculous as the people that stood in them. We all stood in line, grabbing our genitals and clinching our butt cheeks together, hoping we would reach our turn at the toilet before we experienced a personal biohazard disaster. Willpower did not guarantee that you'd actually make it in time, which caused many people to take matters into their own hands to avoid shitting their pants. Given the profound funk I experienced that day, I'm surprised this many people cared whether they shit their pants or not.

Nevertheless, this group didn't care where they took a shit. I saw one man take a shit in a trash can in front of the rest stop. There were obviously many people who were disgusted by this man's actions, but many felt inspired to do the same. Then there were those who just decided to take dumps in random places around the rest area. Several people took a shit in the parking lot, others in the sand at the children's playground, and the rest dropped a deuce out in the grass out by the rest area picnic tables.

When we first arrived at this rest area, it was filled with un-suspecting tourists and happy people on vacation. None of these seemingly normal people had any idea of the malevolence that ascended on this place when we all showed up, but they would quickly learn. There was a large caravan of people going to a family reunion who appeared to be the most traumatized by this mayhem. There were grandpas and grandmas, wives and husbands, uncles and aunts, nieces and nephews, brothers and sisters, and the children... oh... those poor children. Unfortunately, after this shitty experience, no one in the family even understood how they were related anymore, so the whole damn family reunion had to be canceled.

As for my personal experience, it was nothing short of pure hell. I don't know how many people have ever experienced a penguin shit walk before, but I was one of them after coming to this rest area. This is when you clench your butt cheeks so hard you can't really walk. This causes the heels of your feet to come together and your toes to stick out. Then, you just sort of wobble back and forth until you get to the bathroom. You can barely breathe during a penguin shit walk, and you don't really want to because if you exhale too hard, you'll see your life flash before your eyes. Then, if you don't shit your pants or have to throw away your underwear, there is typically a happy dance that follows to celebrate the journey the penguin shit walk took you on. I only know this from watching a few people in front of me. Unfortunately, I didn't do a happy dance that day.

I stood in line behind the massive person that I sat beside on the bus, forestalling nothing short of a natural disaster by the time I reached the shitter. As this time grew near, the fowl stench from the men's rest area continued to get worse and worse. Breathing the toxic fumes was undoubtedly a near-death experience in itself, but sitting in the stall next to the morbidly obese person made me almost have a heart attack.

At this point, I didn't care if I lived or died. I had a metaphoric noose around my neck and was ready to pull it. I just wanted to end it all! The sounds I heard and the putrid smell coming from the man's asshole in the stall next to me made me feel both terrified and angry. I just hoped that I had reached the mountaintop of misery and prayed that it would only get better from here.

Unfortunately, this nightmare got worse... much worse. At some point during this awful experience, I looked over and saw no toilet paper. So, I asked loud enough so everyone in the restroom could hear, "Is there any extra toilet paper in this restroom?" Unfortunately, all I heard was unnerving silence. "Is there any toilet paper at all?" I asked again, but I was answered by another quiet response. This was when the emotions of being terrified and angry intensified, and I think I cried for three straight hours all the way until we reached the Greyhound bus station in San Francisco. This was the shittiest experience in my entire life!

Chapter XI

When I finally arrived at the Greyhound bus station, I felt traumatized yet strangely enthusiastic about my future. I quickly felt happy as I stepped off the bus for a couple of reasons. The most obvious was that the nightmare bus ride was finally over. I was also happy that the bus station was right in the middle of downtown San Francisco. My goal at this point was to find the nearest hotel I could. I was so exhausted from this nightmare that I would have considered sleeping in an alley. Luckily, a Holiday Inn was directly across the street from the station.

I woke up the following day around noon. It was very refreshing to have a nice big bed for myself. I finally got a good night's rest and some privacy after all the craziness I had recently experienced. After eating some lunch, I began to walk around the city for a few hours with no destination in mind until I eventually decided to walk toward the Golden Gate Bridge. There was a road that ran adjacent to the bay where I could look out to see passing ships and Alcatraz Island, which I thought was pretty awesome. I finally made it to my destination by late afternoon and had a spectacular view of this giant red suspension bridge crossing the bay around the time that the sun was beginning to set.

After spending about an hour sightseeing at the Golden Gate Bridge, I started to walk back toward downtown. I found a group of skateboarders somewhere on the way to my motel room and stopped to watch them. They attacked a group of concrete curbs and slants near a sidewalk with all sorts of cool tricks. However, their skateboards narrowly missed the ankles of several people when they crashed, which eventually caused them to be chased off by bicycle police. After this, I continued walking back to my hotel and fell asleep early that night.

After sleeping soundly for twelve hours, I woke up the following morning with a few things on my mind. The first thing I decided to do after breakfast was write an initial email to my nemesis, hoping that he would eventually allow me to purchase Erica's illegal pictures and videos from him. Surprisingly, he replied only a couple of minutes later, which was the first of several conversations I had with him over the next several days. It felt like I gained just a little more of his trust with every email sent. Unfortunately, this didn't seem to get me much closer to removing Erica's pictures and videos from the dark web. I found out that the only currency he would honor was riddled with broken laws and illegal behavior. He explained that I needed to commit specific black-market crimes to help his advancement in the criminal underworld if I ever planned to do any negotiating.

At this point, my journey into his felonious acts of evil wrongdoing had just begun. I would soon learn that this man's illegal realm of wicked plots were endless, and I had no idea how far down this criminal rabbit hole I would need to go to accomplish anything. Although I may not have gained much traction when it came to acquiring Erica's pictures and videos, I did come up with some useful information. It turns out that my nemesis lived in southern

California, which was a convenient coincidence, seeing that I was already on my way to Venice Beach to find my friend, Fredrick.

After this initial email conversation with my nemesis, I planned to call Erica in a desperate attempt to make final amends with her. I hoped that this conversation would lead us back into a committed relationship before she gave Tyler any more blow jobs. I was also interested in knowing if I had outstanding warrants in Nebraska. It would be hard to explain why I wasn't coming home to Erica if I didn't have any warrants.

I came up with the idea to harvest the weed in Nebraska on Billy's farm, but I had not completely wrapped my head around this. All I knew for sure was that my plan needed to include my friend Fredrick. I learned some interesting things about this person when I went with him to the Phish concert earlier in the summer during my failed attempt to move to the West Coast after graduating high school. Unfortunately, I had called Fredrick several times over the past week or so with no answer.

In any case, I planned to convince Erica that the reason for my extended stay on the West Coast was that I was attempting to raise money for her father's heart transplant, which was the truth. I hoped this would allow me to stay on the West Coast and develop more conclusive plans about what I intended to do with all the weed and loot back on Billy's farm. Unfortunately, I predicted that our conversation to be very awkward regardless of how Erica reacted to this information.

The bigger elephant in the room was that we were both having intimate relationships with other people. The ironic thing about this was that I knew that we both truly wanted to be in a committed relationship and were each engaged in these other romantic interests without feeling good about it. At least, I hoped this to be true about her, as I knew this to be true about myself. I had learned my lesson, and if Erica agreed to become my girlfriend again, I was confident I would never engage in any romantic interests other than with her again.

"Hello?"

"Erica, it's me, Oliver."

"I was wondering when the fuck you would call," Erica answered with an angry tone in her voice.

"When were you expecting me to call you back?" I asked, curious about what was making Erica upset.

"The day after the last time you called," she replied.

"But why?" I asked. "I never said I would call you the next day."

"This is true, but I figured you would want to know about your warrants, to see if the coast was clear for your return home, or maybe just to tell me that you loved me... but I guess I was wrong about that!"

At this point, I was vigorously searching for some insightful words to say that would mitigate Erica's anger. I really wanted to offer a reasonable explanation as to why nearly a week had passed since the last time we spoke. I understood the reasons for her anger now, which were deceptively elusive during our previous conversation. I wrongly assumed she expected me to stay on the West Coast longer than a day. Unfortunately, I was at a loss for good excuses and better words while attempting to process the reciprocity in our relationship. "I'm sorry."

"You are sorry?" she replied. "Do you have any idea how many blow jobs I could have given Tyler since the last time we spoke?"

"No," I responded, feeling embarrassed and intimidated.

"I could have given him a metric shit ton of blow jobs, Oliver, but maybe that is what you want," Erica said, with troubling sarcasm.

"No, I don't want that," I responded. "I never want that son of a bitch ever to touch you again!"

"Holy shit, look at Mr. Cassanova trying to serenade me! It's almost like we are in the movie <u>Say Anything</u>, and you are outside my window holding a boombox above your head right now playing "In Your Eyes!" Hold on a few seconds...I will be right back... just let me take a peek outside to see if you're standing outside my window.

"Okay," I responded, completely aware of her cynicism.

I waited in silence for the better part of a minute before Erica finally got back on the phone. "I can't believe it, Oliver, I looked out my window and didn't see you anywhere, which begs the question... WHERE THE FUCK ARE YOU?"

"I'm in San Francisco, holy shit... calm down," I replied, unsuspecting and ready to learn that no woman in history has ever, in fact, calmed down after a man told her to calm down.

"I WILL NOT FUCKING CALM DOWN, OLIVER, AND IF I EVER DO CALM DOWN, IT WILL BE WHEN I AM DAMN GOOD AND READY!" Erica responded, screaming into the phone. This wicked outburst was followed by several seconds of silence before she continued with a more rational tone. "We have been in love since we were eight years old, Oliver. When I was just a little girl, I remember waiting on the front porch for the J.C. Penny catalog to arrive. When it finally showed up, I immediately ran to my room to cut out all the pretty wedding dresses and rings to put into a scrapbook. When I first learned to use the Internet, I didn't know how powerful a search engine was. It never occurred to me to use the internet to help with homework or to write emails. My only interest was to look at wedding rings and wedding dresses.

When I saw you again after four years, it was like I was living in a fairytale. I never told you this, but when we were asked to pick a story in English class to write about, I wrote about Romeo and Juliet because the love described in this story was the kind of love I felt for you! The most beautiful thing about my love for you was that I thought you felt the same way about me. You spent hours writing love letters and poems for me, and I have spent hours making scrapbooks of all these love letters and poems, even those you gave me most recently. Do you have any idea how much time I have spent making scrapbooks and fantasizing about our wedding day?"

"No," I replied, "but I bet it is a lot."

"You are goddamned right it's a lot!" Erica said, with a soft loving voice, "I love you so much that I think that it would be impossible for anyone to love someone more than I love you, and I thought your feelings were the same for me, Oliver, but I don't know anymore. You didn't come home to Ogallala. You didn't call me. You don't even seem to mind that I'm giving Tyler blow jobs. Do you even care about me at all?"

"Yes," I answered. "I care about you."

"That's good, Oliver, because I was just about to let Tyler FUCK ME IN MY ASS!" Erica screamed these four words into the phone receiver so loud that it hurt my ear. I'm not talking metaphorically as if my feelings were hurt. I mean, my right ear actually hurt for a couple of days following this conversation.

"Erica, please listen to me," I replied. "The way you love me is exactly the same way that I love you, and I do plan to marry you someday."

"What the hell are you doing in San Francisco then?" Erica asked. "Why are you there and not here with me?"

"I can explain."

"Go right ahead," she replied. "This better be good."

"I'm in San Francisco on my way to southern California to find my friend, Fredrick."

"You mean the same Fredrick with ten million hits of acid and a bazillion bags of weed in his van... the hippy that brought you to a Phish concert... is that the Fredrick you are talking about?" Erica asked.

"Yes, that Fredrick." I replied.

"So, you want to hang out with your hippy friend more than me?"

"No," I replied. "Just listen to me."

"Okay, I'll listen but you better choose your words very carefully because if you tell me that you're going with Fredrick on a Phish tour, I will cut your fucking dick off!"

This is when I just took a deep breath and started talking without thinking, "When I found out that your dad was dying and that you were so determined to figure out a way to get your dad a heart transplant that you somehow ended up on the dark web, I didn't know what to think. I mean, I was impressed that you actually figured out how to navigate your way onto the dark web and then found a place on the black market to get your dad an illegal transplant... but mostly, I just felt really pissed off that you let a man exploit you for information... I mean, I wasn't mad at you... I was super pissed at the man that you were talking to. Then, when I accidentally called you a slut... I mean, when you thought I called you a slut, but that wasn't what I really meant... but then, you got super mad at me anyways and told me to leave, so I did, and then, I sat on your front steps with your computer crying... and then, when I sat there, I began to realize how much your dad meant to you because I know that you'd never do something like get naked on the internet unless it was literally a life or death situation. Then, I even got more upset at the evil man that took advantage of your incredibly vulnerable feelings when it came to trying to save your dad, then, I thought some more and made it my life's goal to find a way to pay for your dad's heart transplant, and then, I wanted to kill that son of a bitch that made you take off your clothes. I swear to God, if I ever find that man, I will throw him into a pig pen till the pigs eat his dick. I'm going to rip his head off and shit down his throat. I hate that motherfucker! Then, Adam killed that fat kid at his party, and ... and ... and I almost had sex with that girl in the park because I was super drunk and sad that you were mad at me. Then, you called me the next day, and I was super happy, but then, you found out that I fucked around with a football player's girlfriend... and then, you got really mad at me again, then... me and Billy ate mushrooms and got really fucked up, and Billy got even more fucked up, and... he ran into a minivan that almost killed an entire family. Now, Billy is a vegetable, and I went to jail, and the police wanted me to rat on my friends, so I decided to just leave rather than deal with my legal problems, but then... I went to Billy's house to look for his money because I didn't want the police to find it. I found five bags of weed, and tons, and tons of guns, and a whole bunch of money... and I didn't know what to do. So, I took some money and buried everything in a giant hole under your old house… and … and … and it took me two days to dig this hole. Then, I saw you at the supermarket, and you looked really sad. I didn't want to leave you. I left because I thought I needed to. I went to Las Vegas, and Portland, and Seattle… and I talked to you, but I didn't know that you wanted me to come home because you were giving Tyler blow jobs, and I didn't know what to do, but then, I started to come up with a whole bunch of plans to come back to Nebraska to dig up the money under your old house to buy Adam and Billy a good lawyer, and now I'm trying to figure out a way to save Billy's farm… and think I have figured out how to get most of the money for your dad's heart transplant… because the most important thing in the world to me is to make you happy, and I know that you'd be really sad if your dad died, and thought how he couldn't walk you down the aisle at our wedding when we get married, so now I plan to harvest the weed out in the field at Billy's farm and sell it, but this whole plan of mine won't work unless I find Fredrick… so now I'm going to his house to try to find him…"

"Stop, Oliver, just stop for a second," Erica said, promptly interrupting my crazy-ass rambling excuses. "Did you just say that you have a plan to raise most of the money for my father's heart transplant?"

"I haven't figured it all out yet, but yes, I think I have a plan," I answered.

"Do you really think that you have figured out how to get over a million dollars?" Erica asked in disbelief.

"Maybe not over a million dollars, but … well… maybe, yeah," I answered.

"You do?" Erica asked, whose demeanor had now changed from one of anger to one of someone completely dumbfounded.

"Yes, I do," I answered.

"Would you mind reviewing this plan with a little more detail?" Erica asked.

"Okay, so when Billy and I were out fishing one day, he told me that he planted a bigger field of marijuana this year."

"How much more weed could he possibly plant?"

"A lot more... like way, way, way more... enough to possibly pay for your dad's heart transplant," I answered, stretching the truth a bit from both sides. If my plan worked perfectly, I figured the weed could be sold for about three-quarters of a million dollars. However, this was just a guess and a generous one at that. I also had no other plans at this point. However, while walking mindlessly into this abyss of half-truths, I was highly hopeful I'd figure out a plan to get the rest of the money.

"Why exactly do you need to find Fredrick?" Erica asked. "You said your plan won't work without him...why?"

"I don't know how to harvest marijuana. I also have no idea where to sell that much weed, but I am pretty sure Fredrick does," I answered. "Billy always had some secret deal worked out with one of the farmers around here to help him harvest... and I guess he has customers all over the state, but I don't know anyone to sell weed to besides a few high school students. He never told me much about any of this until we went fishing a couple of weeks before his accident. I was just happy that he always gave me free weed and bought booze all the time. I didn't get into his business. I had no idea how much weed he grew or where he sold it. I just thought he sold all of his pot to high school students and people at the bowling alley bar."

"Okay, wait a minute... back up here, so what exactly did Billy say to you while you were out fishing," Erica asked, seeming incredibly interested in what I had to say about all this.

"I asked him if he ever planned to move away from Nebraska, and he told me that he did, but needed to save more money. I asked how much money he planned to save, and that's how I found out Billy had already saved up over two hundred thousand dollars. He said he grew three hundred pounds of weed last year and planted over a thousand plants this year. Billy told me that he spent over five grand to purchase high-quality seeds from someone in Humboldt County, California."

"Isn't that the place that you and your hippy friend picked up all those trash bags full of weed?" Erica asked. "The place where you saw a pile of weed the size of a house?"

"Yep, that's the same place," I answered. "I never really thought about that before."

"How much weed do you think comes from five thousand dollars of marijuana seeds?"

"I don't know for sure," I answered. "This is one of the questions I plan to ask Fredrick, but think it might be enough to buy your dad a new heart."

"Are you telling me the truth about all this?"

"Yes, to the best of my knowledge... I swear to God that I am," I answered.

"And this is why you need to find your hippy friend, Fredrick?" Erica asked, seeming to put the last piece of the puzzle together.

"Yes," I answered, sighing with relief that Erica seemed to understand my story and wasn't mad at me anymore.

"So, the reason you are out on the West Coast right now and not home with me is only because you want to buy my dad a new heart?" Erica asked, as her voice suddenly became impeccably seductive.

"There is that, but I also love you too much to come home right now," I replied.

"How so?" Erica asked. "That makes no sense."

"I've been thinking about this, and I'm sure we will spend the rest of our lives together once I return home, but if I come home now, I won't be able to save your dad's life," I answered. "Then, he won't be there to walk you down the aisle when we get married. Every time you have described our wedding day, it has always included your father walking you down the aisle."

"We can get married this fall," she replied with a sexually alluring tone.

"Is that what you want?" I asked, shocked that she would suggest this after how mad she had been only minutes earlier.

"I don't know what I want, but I think I just fell even more in love with you just now, and I didn't think that was possible," she said, "and your big heart just made me super horny all of a sudden. If you were here on my bed with me right now, I'd let you do anything you wanted to me."

"Anything?"

"Pretty close," Erica responded.

"Really?"

"Yes, really," she replied. Around this time, I started hearing a buzzing sound in the background.

"So, what's going on with my warrants?"

"I talked to your mom the other day... hold on for a second," Erica said. For about thirty seconds, I just heard low-volume sounds of female sexual pleasure.

"Erica, so what did my mom say?" I asked, continuing to listen to Erica vigorously playing with herself.

"I told her where you were at, and she... hold on, just give me a few more seconds," Erica replied, while listening to a steady rhythm of sexual pleasure increase in intensity. I never had phone sex or anything like it before this conversation, so I didn't know what to do. I knew that everyone masturbated, but it wasn't something we openly talked about much at our age unless we were joking. I felt really embarrassed by all this at the time. However, if I had known then what I know now, I would have jumped right in with some dirty talk and rubbed one out myself.

"Hey, do I still have warrants?" I continued to ask.

"All you have is a misdemeanor possession of marijuana," Erica blurted out, which was immediately followed by a very loud moan, indicating a substantial step toward climax. "Oh my God, Oliver, I want your cock so bad right now."

"What the hell are you doing?" I asked, knowing exactly what she was doing.

"I'm imagining that your... oh God... oh God..."

"What are you imagining?" I asked.

"I'm imagining that your... oh fuck me, oh God."

"What, are you trying..."

"I'M IMAGINING THAT I'M GETTING FUCKING PLOWED," Erica yelled before lowering her voice. "I'm on my bed with my ass up, and I have a dildo buried so far inside me it's hard to talk. I am imagining that you are behind me, absolutely destroying my pussy! Oliver, will you please shut up and just let me finish!"

Over the next minute or two, I heard Erica make some of the craziest sexual sounds I had ever heard. I thought that if she had this much fun alone, I must have been doing something wrong the past two years. Suddenly, I heard her scream, FUCK YES, OLIVER!" after hearing a loud, high-pitched squeal of fantastic sexual pleasure, indicating she had reached a climax."

After several seconds passed, listening to her breath slowing in frequency, I asked, "So, can you talk now?"

"Not really... no... call me later," she said.

"Okay, but before you go, I want to know two things."

"What?" she asked, seeming to be slightly annoyed.

"Do you want me to go find Fredrick or come home?"

"Mmmm... you decide... I trust that you will do what's best for us."

"Does this mean you are my girlfriend again?" I asked, desperately hoping she would say yes.

"I'm SOOOoooooo your girlfriend again, Oliver, you have no idea," she answered.

"Awesome," I replied, as this call promptly ended. As weird as this conversation was, it deeply affected my decision-making moving forward. I was particularly relieved when this roller-coaster ride of emotions was finally over. After processing this conversation, I was particularly interested in Erica's answers to the last two questions I asked. They were each profound in vastly different ways. The fact that she had just become my girlfriend again had obvious reasons to make me happy, which anyone could easily understand.

However, her other statement, which indicated that she trusted me to do what was best for us, was more of a puzzle to solve. I would move forward through life, often thinking about these very words. It may come as no surprise to learn that Erica and I would spend the rest of our lives together. There wasn't a time that we ever discussed a significant break in our relationship again. The sanctity of our commitment was so strong that infidelity was never something that either one of us had to think about again. Every decision I made would be for us moving into the future. The enigma of perfect decision-making regarding our relationship would never be completely solved. However, I will continue to answer this riddle for the rest of my life.

Chapter XII

AFTER LEAVING MY HOTEL room that morning, I made it a point to visit Fisherman's Wharf, Chinatown, and the intersection of Haight and Ashbury. I thought this city was unique, except for the overabundance of homeless people. Coming from rural Nebraska, I had nothing to compare this experience to, but I found it odd that San Francisco had such a large homeless population.

I was still unsure about what I wanted to do for a living, but I knew I didn't want to end up homeless. My short-term goals included a trip to Los Angeles. As for now, I was enjoying my time in San Francisco, even if it would only be for a couple of days. That afternoon, I found San Francisco to be a beautiful and enlightening city in which to spend time. The buildings that shaped the city skyline had a surreal design to them. I thought that this was a fascinating and beautiful city to be in.

In the evening, I went to a coffee shop to ponder my next move and to finish drawing a picture that I had started on the bus ride from hell. I felt inspired by the picture that I drew in Seattle and decided to create a sequel. I had nearly finished this picture when a kid in his early twenties approached me.

"Hey man, do you have a cigarette?" he asked.

"No, sorry, I don't have any," I replied.

I didn't think much about this interaction and went back to drawing a picture, but this kid continued to hover above me, watching me draw. A few minutes passed before I looked at this kid and asked, "What do you think?"

"Your picture is awesome," he said. "Where do you get your ideas?"

"I don't know, really... they just sort of come to me."

I finished my drawing and was about to leave the coffee shop when I saw the same kid standing over my shoulder again, "It's all finished," I said. "What do you think?"

"That's great work!"

"Thank you," I replied. "My name is Oliver."

"I'm Brian."

"What are you doing at the coffee shop?" I asked. "You've been here for a while."

"I just thought it would probably be a good idea to get as much caffeine in me as possible. We are headed to an all-night party that's supposed to be off the chain! I'm just preparing myself for a long night."

"Where is the party at?"

"I don't know exactly... downtown, somewhere? My friend Eric over there has got the details. We have room in the car if you want to come along. Why don't you come to our table to meet some of my friends, and I will ask them if it's cool."

"Okay," I replied.

Then, I closed my notebook and followed Brian to the table where his friends were sitting. Brian purposely turned his back toward me as he discussed the party with one of his friends. Although his friend didn't seem overjoyed with me coming along, Brain continued with his original invite to what sounded like a decent party. "Do you want to come along?"

"Does it cost anything?" I asked with high hopes of him saying no.

"The only thing that it is going to cost you is the possibility that Justin isn't as good of a friend with the guy throwing the party as he claims," Brian said. "In which case, the information that he was told to get through security was completely bunk and would result in none of us getting in, so there is a slight chance it will cost you a bit of bullshit."

His friend, who I assumed to be Justin, replied. "I never said I knew the person throwing the party. I said that I had four guest list spots because my brother's production company does sound for his parties."

"Okay then," Brian responded.

"I am on the guest list to his parties and pretty much any party in this city that is worth going to," Justin interrupted, with a cocky attitude. "My name will get you on the guest list to get in, so don't fuck up. I suggest to not get drunk and make an ass out of yourselves. You fuck up here, and you will never be invited back. As for you," Justin said, turning toward me, "Even though I don't know you, I will say for certain that this party will blow your mind!"

"Whatever..." the girl sitting across from Justin said. "If you were as hooked up as you say you are, then how come we don't go to all the cool parties with all the cool people and get all the cool drugs for free? We have only been to one of these parties your brother supposedly hooks you up with. It was pretty cool and all, but I'm waiting to see if you can pull this off again."

Before this statement was made, I didn't hear this girl say anything. I thought she was a shy person that didn't say much. I guess I thought wrong. Although I was uncertain if she was kidding, I'd never seen a more serious face in my life. Feeling a bit shy, it took a moment of confidence to ask her, "What's your name?"

"My name is Dawn," she said. "I'm sorry you are getting sucked into this, and I will apologize ahead of time for my friends being dumb shits."

"Hey, Oliver, are you going to come with us, or what?" Brian asked.

"Yeah, I'll come along with you," I told him, eager to see what I was getting myself into. I probably wouldn't have gone with them if I had based my decision solely on Dawn or Justin's description of the party. However, Brian seemed like a kid I wanted to get to know, so I didn't figure there was anything to lose. It's not like I had something better to do.

Eric rode shotgun, and I sat in the back with Dawn while Brian drove us to this party. His vehicle was an older model VW bug from the 1960s, which made this car ride very unpleasant. The party was in Los Angeles, and it took nearly an hour to get there. Unfortunately, the bumps in the road and being crammed in the back of this ridiculously compact car caused me to get sick just as we began to fly by the skyscrapers of downtown LA. Eventually, this ill feeling of car sickness got so bad that I thought that I'd vomit before we made it to our destination. The last thing I wanted to do was puke all over

Dawn and the back seat of Brian's car, so I finally decided to speak up about the unsettling feeling in my stomach before I started to blow chunks, "Hey, dude, if we don't get somewhere pretty quickly, I think I might hurl."

"We will be there in a few," Brian replied. "If you have to puke, I will pull over."

"How much further is it?" I asked, envisioning myself puking my guts out all over Dawn.

"Only a block or two," Justin said, and we arrived at our destination within a minute. I was relieved as Justin told Brian to turn into an underground parking garage beneath a skyscraper in the middle of downtown. I was rather impressed that Justin knew precisely where we were going. After we parked the car, we took an escalator to the main floor. When we arrived at this level, we were immediately met by a couple of intimidating security officers. However, Justin showed him some tickets, and we were allowed in.

The inside of the building we entered was substantially more interesting than the outside. A skywalk connected one side of the building to another, while a group of elevators connected the bottom floor to the top. Creative interior design covered the walls and floors, and large pieces of artwork were everywhere I looked.

The front desk we walked toward to get to this party was made of just one giant chunk of polished marble in the middle of an enormous lobby. Behind this chunk of marble sat a gorgeous woman. She was very polite when asking what she could help us with. Justin told this lady that we were on the guest list for the party and wanted to know how to find it. Then, she asked for our IDs and tickets at this point, and after showing her our credentials, she directed us toward elevators. "It's on the fifty-seventh floor," she said. "You can't miss it."

Finally, we reached the party, and my immediate opinion was that it was above and beyond what Brian described. I became more than impressed as we began to walk around. We followed Justin as he searched for his brother. At first, we all stuck together, but eventually, Brian and I went our separate ways from Justin and Dawn. Eventually, we wandered over to a punch bowl and grabbed a drink.

The party was nothing like I had ever seen before. There was a DJ playing techno and a large group of people dancing around in front of him. Everyone looked like they were having a great time. Even if you weren't into music, you could probably find someone interesting to talk to in the crowd of two or three hundred people. Also, the view was amazing. This floor offered nearly a 360-degree view of the city skyline. This alone would be worth coming to the party.

"What do you think of this party?" Brian asked.

"It's pretty cool. I had no idea that it was going to be like this. I was picturing a smaller house party or something. Did you know it was going to be this awesome?" I asked.

"I didn't know it would be this big, but I'm familiar with the venue and knew it would be pretty elaborate compared to a house party."

"Did you know how awesome this building was going to be?"

"Yeah, we came to a party here a couple of months ago, but even if I saw it a million times, it would still blow my mind that we are actually at a party near the top floor. I couldn't believe how nice this place was when I first came here," Brian said. "The first time we were here, we were expecting a studio in a high-rise, not an entire floor. I have heard numerous rumors that the man who threw this party owns this entire building!"

"Wow, I can't believe someone could even own a building like this," I said to Brian, whose attention was now partially concentrated on an attractive girl beside him. "What does he use the rest of the building for?"

"It's mostly used for research or something, but I don't really know. I don't even know if any of the rumors are true," Brian said in between a conversation he had started with the girl beside him. He quickly made it clear that he was conversing with this woman and that our little chat was over, and the first time I had my back toward him, he seemed to disappear.

I was now standing alone and felt lost, not having anyone to talk to in the middle of a large crowd. I had no idea where any of my new friends were. Although the party was fantastic, being a country boy, I couldn't entirely relate to the party vibe. Then, after about ten minutes of feeling awkward, I noticed the same girl that Brian was flirting with standing directly in front of me on the dance floor, so I tapped her on the shoulder and asked, "Hey, where did Brian go?"

"Who's Brian?" she asked.

"My friend that you were talking to a little bit ago."

"I have no idea who you are talking about," she said. "Do you know who the DJ is?"

"I don't know," I answered. "I don't listen to much electronic music."

"That's too bad," she said with a smile. "This music is good for your soul."

"Right on, maybe I'll try dancing a bit later," I replied.

"I hope you find your friend," she said, before dancing into the crowd.

"Me too!"

Moments later, I noticed Justin sitting on an oversized fluffy couch next to a guy rolling a joint, so I decided to sit beside him. At first, he didn't say anything to me. He just kept doing his own thing. I thought that maybe he was ignoring me, but after about a minute or so had passed, Justin finally asked, "Are you having fun?" As he said this, I could tell in his voice that he wasn't too excited about me sitting next to him. I got the feeling that he didn't like me very much. I didn't understand why, but I didn't care either. I had nowhere to go, so he would have to deal with my company for a while.

"Yeah, this is a great party," I answered.

"Is it what you expected?" Justin asked.

"Everything, and a lot more, this venue is incredible. It's also pretty trippy looking out of the windows."

"Yeah, wait till the punch you're drinking kicks in."

"Why, it's pretty weak," I replied. "I don't even taste any alcohol."

"Didn't you notice the sign over the punch bowl that read LSD?" Justin said with a smirk on his face.

"Holy shit, no, I didn't," I replied. "I thought it was alcohol!"

"How much did you drink?" Eric asked.

"Almost two glasses," I said, looking in my cup to see that my second glass was mostly empty.

"You'll be all right. That's equivalent to only a couple of hits, and it's intentionally super weak acid. If you want some alcohol, it's sitting right over there," he responded, pointing toward a bar with a crowd of people standing in front of it.

"I'm not twenty-one," I replied, alluding the fact that I had a fake ID. This caused Justin and a heavy-set man next to him to start laughing.

"Man, you really don't know where you're at, do you?"

"No, I guess I don't. Where am I?" I responded, which caused Justin and the heavy-set guy to roar with laughter.

A joint was soon passed my way, and I took a couple of hits before passing it back to Justin. As I watched a cloud of smoke roll out of Justin's mouth, he introduced me to the man beside him, "Oliver, this is my brother, Joe."

"Oh, so you're the guy Justin was talking about," I replied, looking at Joe.

"I don't know," he replied. "What did Joe have to say about me?"

"He just said that his brother would be at this party... that's all."

"I guess if that's all he said, I'm not going to have to kick his ass... although he probably deserves it," Joe replied, as he punched his brother on the arm a couple of times. "No, really, man... you're more than welcome to drink or smoke... whatever you want. Just ask the bartender. It's all free!"

"Really?" I responded.

"Yeah, man, go for it. The guy who is throwing this party is stupid rich. It's all on the house."

"Thanks for the info!" I replied as I sat up from a cloud of smoke.

After getting up and walking around for a bit, I found my way over to the punch bowl again, and sure enough, there was a sign that said "LSD." This led me to think that I was about to start tripping on acid. However, at no point in the night did I ever really feel like I was tripping. I knew what the effects of good acid were after meeting my friend, Fredrick, so it was easy to determine that this acid was either incredibly weak or not LSD at all.

Eventually, I wandered up to the bar. "What will it be?" the bartender asked.

"A dirty martini," I answered, not knowing what it was or if I would like it. I only ordered this drink because I always wondered what James Bond was drinking during all of his movies.

"Gin or vodka?"

"Gin," I replied.

"How many Olives do you want?" the bartender asked as I watched him fill a martini glass with top-shelf gin and olive juice.

"A couple, I guess!" I responded, hoping that was an appropriate number of olives to add to a martini.

At this point in the night, it was still early, maybe only ten o'clock. For the next couple of hours, I mainly stood around the bar nursing Martinis. I had no real intention of getting drunk because I didn't want to lose my new friends, and I also just wasn't feeling up to it. I occasionally saw Brian, Dawn, Joe, and Justin walking around, but I never really engaged in much conversation for the remainder of my time at this party.

Around midnight, I started to notice an awful lot of people leaving, which I found to be strange. At least half the people were high on drugs, so they were not leaving this party to go home and sleep. Around this time, Brian found me and discussed going to another party. Although he called it a party, what he described was a rave.

Coming from rural Nebraska, I felt out of place with this particular culture. Nevertheless, I decided to go with him and his friends because I had nothing better to do. Also, somewhere in my mind, I thought I would return to Nebraska soon and may never have the opportunity to go to a rave again. Hence, the element of life experience was also present in my decision to go to a rave.

After leaving this initial party, we had to call a number on the rave flyer to get some information. Then, we drove to a record store downtown called a map point. This place was accurately named because that is where we acquired a second set of directions, which would lead to the party itself. We showed up at the rave about an hour later, and it was a lot like I predicted it to be.

The rave was inside a large warehouse, and there was a long line to get inside. The people who stood in this line were wearing giant pants called Jnco and Kickwear. Some of these kids wore a variety of rainbow-beaded necklaces around their necks and bracelets around their wrists. In the short time we spent in this line, we were also inundated with people handing out flyers to future raves.

I had an opportunity to look at the flyer of the party we attended that night, which explained several details. I guess this particular party was much larger than most. There were three giant rooms where DJs would play different varieties of electronic dance music. There was one room called "Drum and Bass" where Diesel Boy, Roni Size, DJ Craze, and DJ Dara were headlining. Then, another room called "House" where Mark Farina, Doc Martin, Sunshine Jones, and Donald Glaude were headlining, and finally, there was the "Main Stage" where Rabbit in the Moon, Sasha, and Digweed would play extended sets of their music.

I remember being approached multiple times by people selling different types of designer drugs. As they delivered their sales pitch, always claiming to be selling potent drugs, I realized that drugs were a significant part of the rave culture. This aspect reminded me of the hippy culture I had experienced at the Phish Concert. Many of the same drugs I saw at the Phish concert were also being sold here. The LSD being sold was in the form of microdots, gel tabs, liquid, and blotter paper, and it was far from weak acid. There was also an array of ecstasy, molly, and ketamine floating around. Brian and his friends didn't buy any drugs while waiting in line, but they made it clear that they intended to take ecstasy at some point during the night. They mentioned knowing a guy on the inside who sold the best quality of this particular drug.

Once we all finally got inside, I looked around the main room and was amazed by all the lights and massive stacks of speakers. The DJ booth had all sorts of electronic equipment, including four record players and a mixer in the middle. It was also very cool to watch the dancers. The DJ table was very elaborate compared to the smaller rooms, where the DJ booth was created by a wooden board that sat on top of cement cinder blocks. The smaller rooms also only had two turntables.

As Brian, his friends, and I walked around, it would not be long before they found the drug dealer they were looking for. There was very little discretion regarding the fact that he sold drugs. This was not to the extent of the people at the Phish concert, who had signs made to describe the drugs they had for sale, but it was still pretty noticeable. In any case, we each paid him twenty dollars, and he gave us all little white pills called a Mitsubishi, which actually had the Mitsubishi trademark pressed into it.

After taking a good look at this pill of ecstasy, we all ate them at the same time. Then, we walked around again for half an hour or so. Once the ecstasy began to kick in, Brian, Dawn, and myself were unintentionally separated from Justin and his brother. Fifteen minutes later, not a single one of us could stand up.

This is when we found ourselves in one of the many groups of people who sat on the floor, experiencing exactly what I experienced that night. These groups of people were referred to as a "cuddle puddle." Brian, Dawn, and I sat on the side of a cuddle puddle that initially only consisted of about thirty people. However, this cuddle puddle grew to about two hundred people within an hour. I figured the reason for this was that we likely ate our drugs around the same time.

The individuals in this group were extremely social. I saw that their mouths were making strange movements while they were speaking and even when they were not. Many of them had tongue piercings, which added to the unusual behaviors of their mouths. To cope with this, some people sucked on baby pacifiers, others chewed gum, some smoked cigarettes, and others had ring pops or suckers.

The drug itself was incredibly pleasant. Everyone sat around giving each other massages, and I experienced a rolling ecstasy feeling that lasted about three hours. The cuddle puddles started disappearing around three or four in the morning. This was because the effects of the drug switched gears and made you want to dance. At this point in the night, you felt a strong desire to dance regardless of what drug you were on. Some people at this rave were outstanding dancers and moved their bodies in ways I never knew were possible. A small group of dancers also incorporated lights into their dance movements. I walked through every room a few times, dancing around, and eventually spent the rest of the night in the room called "house."

The rave finally ended about the same time that the sun was rising. As we exited the warehouse, everyone looked really fucked up, and they all seemed to be scrambling to find an after-party. I couldn't believe that there was yet another party to go to. I discovered that it was not uncommon for these kids to begin to party on Friday night and then continuously party till Sunday afternoon. Remarkably, they would be ready for work or school on Monday and then do it again the following weekend.

After I felt that my mission was accomplished for the night, I said goodbye to my raver friends and called a cab to take me to the nearest hotel. As I sat in the hotel, I felt a very odd feeling of sickness in my entire body, especially in my head and stomach. This was the worst part of my experience with ecstasy. I had similar feelings with mushrooms and acid around the eighth hour into the trip. I believe that consuming more drugs can extend the enjoyable aspects of these substances. It's also possible to lessen the undesirable ending with benzodiazepine or alcohol. However, there is no way to completely avoid the negative effects of drugs.

Picture drawn at the coffee shop.

Chapter XIII

I SPENT THE NEXT twenty-four hours in my hotel room recovering and planned to continue traveling to southern California the following day. Before I left the Bay Area, I visited one of the city's many art museums on Mission Street in the middle of downtown. I was not impressed with this art museum at all. I disliked it so much that I gained a new respect for the museum I visited in Portland. Later in life, after visiting art museums around the globe, I realized that my opinion of these museums was jaded by the fact that I was a young kid from rural Nebraska who had little cultural exposure while growing up.

I learned that you need to relax and understand that your opinions don't amount to anything. Why be a critic if you are not being paid to criticize? There is no point in complaining about things other people enjoy just because you have different interests. Moreover, you often come across as ignorant or, worse yet, an asshole.

Despite everything I would later learn about art and culture, my opinions on this particular day remained unchanged. I thought that San Francisco would probably have a decent art museum since it was a big city known for its random beauty and architecture. In my youthful opinion, it had four stories of mostly nonsense. The majority of the artwork in this museum were these giant installations that appeared to have been made by a bunch of random things out of junk left next to city dumpsters.

By default, every piece of art I looked at, I immediately thought, "This is stupid!" At one point, I found myself observing what I thought to be a particularly shitty work of art. I stood in front of a bunch of shapes hanging from the ceiling. Then, I observed four rectangular bars hanging behind some circular and triangular pieces of metal. This was set in front of a black canvas and hung over hundreds of little metal spikes varying in length poking out of the floor.

After a brief gander, I felt satisfied with my opinion and decided to carry on my intentions to leave the building. However, one man stood between me and the exit of that museum. Ironically, for the next several minutes, he and I would converse about the concept of art. He was a young man wearing a second-hand suit who didn't appear to be much older than I was. He was twisting his head and crossing his brow, attempting to understand this piece.

"Do you understand this piece?" this man asked just before I was prepared to leave.

"No, and I don't really care to," I answered.

"Why is that?" he asked. "Don't you like the piece?"

"No, in fact, I don't like very much of anything in this museum!"

"I love this place," the man said, holding out his hand for a polite and formal introduction. "My name is Thad."

"My name is Oliver."

"Nice to meet you," he reciprocated, seeming cheerful as hell. I could see an odd glow from the excitement Thad was experiencing while visiting this art museum. Essentially, I believed that he was feeling the exact opposite of myself. The look on his face expressed a notion that he wanted to tell the world about what he was thinking, and ... well... here I was standing beside him. "Have you seen the artwork on the third floor?" Thad asked.

"Yeah! That floor sucked donkey balls! The worthless junk I saw on that floor was even worse than this floor. I think that part of the museum, in particular, probably creates one of the largest collections of stupid shit I have ever seen," I said, expressing how down my opinion of this museum was.

"WOW!" Thad responded. Our contrasting opinions put him on the brink of yelling as he began to tell me what he was thinking. "We must have very different views about art because I like this place so much that I come here once a month just to look at this work of art we are standing in front of. It is magnificent! I could only imagine what the artist was thinking while creating this piece...

I believe the spikes represent fear of sorts, like fear of falling, perhaps metaphysically, into the jagged edges of life. All of these shapes are suspended and cannot move any closer to the sharp points of metal because of the wire that suspends them. Yet, they can be moved in any other direction. The shapes can even touch each other if pushed together, but they cannot escape the radius of the wire that suspends them. This radius could be interpreted as the world and the reality to which we are bound...

The four rectangular pieces in the back tell the story of an average person, ordinary in every way. Together, the four pieces in the back also represent strength and pride because they are alike and needed to complete this piece. The shapes in front have character and are much larger than the ones in the back. They are more robust and admired in contrast to the shapes behind them. Yet, they also remain motionless. I believe that the spikes themselves represent pain and suffering. They keep a constant reminder that life is hard on everyone."

I couldn't believe that he got all of that from this gigantic hunk of shit. I didn't know how to respond to this. I didn't want to offend him because he seemed serious about his perspective. Rather than explain my honest opinion to him, I passively and quietly responded, "Yep, I would have to say that we definitely have different opinions about what art is."

"Oh, and why is that?" Thad asked.

"Because I don't think this is art at all," I answered. "Art is different to me."

"How so?" Thad asked. "How would you explain art?"

"I don't know... I guess it would be like defining what art means to me and then making my own creations or something." I responded.

"I would describe it as discovering the truth behind one's imagination," Thad said, as if to prove that he understood the concepts of art better than me. "Artistically speaking... however, the dictionary definition is a human skill of expressing other objects by painting, drawing, sculpting, etc. In this case, the expression of other objects would be metal."

"How do you figure?" I asked. "What object is being expressed here?"

"With this piece, you must extend the definition of art by including the expression of emotion and concepts. When you draw or paint, do you always create an object you see, or can you envision something original?"

"I draw pictures of objects that I envision myself for the most part," I answered.

"Within these objects, do you believe that the foundation of your artwork is to create emotion or even a concept of your own?"

"I guess so," I answered reluctantly, unsure I even understood his brainy question.

"I truly believe that the foundation of art is found in emotion, making it impossible to limit such a vast concept to tangible things," Thad responded. "What sort of art do you do?"

"I draw, and I write poetry mostly," I replied. "What about you?"

"I write non-fiction stories and news articles about sports for an LA area news station."

"What the fuck?" I responded, expressing a look of confusion.

"Yes, it is," Thad replied, expressing a solid conviction for his work.

By this time, I had figured out that Thad was pretty clever. I realized by now that he was just as smart as I was, or even more intelligent, but something was very different between us. It had nothing to do with the fact that he was standing in this museum wearing a cheap suit, and I was standing beside him wearing baggy shorts with a Propagandi band shirt I bought at the concert in Portland. I felt that we were different in a very fundamental aspect, but I couldn't quite put my finger on it.

Also, I know this was an exciting time in the history of America. It had been over two decades since America fought in Vietnam, and it was just before the war in Iraq. It seemed that this was a time when racism and homophobias were put on a peculiar shelf for a little while. This was long after the freedoms of black folks were made the same as white folks, at least according to law. During this time in history, gay people finally felt safe to come out of the closet. It was before Obama and Trump became president, and so the people who were racist or homophobic didn't speak up as much to express their opinions. People had more of a tendency to listen to the most intelligent person in the room rather than the one who spoke the loudest.

Strangely enough, by this point in the conversation, we seemed to have formed a mutual respect for each other's opinions and intelligence. That is probably why the conversation continued. However, rather than discussing our views of art, we began a battle of wits. At the beginning of the conversation, Thad appeared to take the perspective of a conservative person, and I took on the argument of more of a liberal. Our original conversation was constructed from the concepts of art but eventually led toward a different direction.

"What makes you a conservative person?" I asked.

"What do you mean... a conservative person?" Thad responded with a look of surprise.

"With your suit and tie... that sort of thing."

"That is kind of a strange question... and a rather hard one to answer," Thad replied, twisting his head and grabbing his chin. "Mmmm... First, it might be appropriate to define what I think being a conservative means... I guess the basis for being a conservative is stability, and the basis for liberalism is change. If I have any conservative tendencies, they only relate to the goals I hold. Everything in my life, at least since I graduated from high school, has revolved around certain short-term and long-term goals, and I always try to preserve those goals by keeping a consistent character.

Strangely enough, I see myself being a more liberal person, and I see you being more conservative."

"I wouldn't call myself a conservative at all," I said, with a cross look on my face. "I travel and live on almost nothing. Look at my band shirt. Propagandi's music is incredibly liberal and expresses hatred for everything conservative. The lead singer is even openly gay!"

"Do you like gay people?" Thad asked, as if it were a trick question.

"Sure, as long as they don't grab my ass or blow kisses at me."

"And, if they did, would you be offended?"

"What I am saying is that they don't bother me if they mind their own business."

"Based on your comments, I gather that you are homophobic?"

"Hell no! They don't scare me. I just let a gay homeless person stay the night in my motel room a couple of weeks ago."

"What if your boss was openly gay?" Thad asked. "Would you be cool with that?"

"I don't have a job," I replied, "so that question wouldn't apply to me."

"Do you ever plan on getting a job?"

"I suppose that I will someday."

"Do you plan on getting married?"

"I guess so."

"Do you plan on living in a house?"

"Yeah, I suppose I do."

"What about children?"

"Where are you going with this?" I asked. "Even if I am fifty, I will still think with an open mind. Even if my position in life changes, most of my views and opinions will not."

"Perhaps your views and opinion should change," Thad stated. "Have you ever thought of that?"

"How so?"

"Maybe some of your views and opinions should be more liberal, and others should be more conservative."

"In the five additional years of life experience you have over me, you think that you have figured out everything... and that you are wise enough to pass judgment on me without even knowing me?" I asked. "I think your analogies are rather shallow, and you are being somewhat arrogant. I think and act freely. That is who I am."

"You may be right," Thad replied.

"I know that I am right!"

"Have you ever read Emerson?"

"I haven't actually."

"You would really like his work. He is one of my favorite authors. I have memorized a passage that I think you could relate to. It is quite possibly my favorite paragraph that Emerson ever wrote. Would you like to hear it?"

"I suppose."

"What I must do is all that concerns me, not what the people think. This rule, equally arduous in actual and intellectual life, may serve the whole distinction between greatness and meanness. It is harder because you will always find those who think they know what your duty is better than you know it. It is easy in this world to live after the world's opinion. It is easy in solitude to live after our own, but the great man is he who in the midst of the crowd keeps with perfect sweetness the independence of solitude."

Ralph Waldo Emerson

"That's awesome!" I responded with new found respect for Thad's intelligence.

"You're a smart, young man, and I'm sure you will do fine in whatever you want to pursue in this world," Thad said.

"Right on, you have an interesting perspective about art. I didn't really want to get down on your opinions. I was just disappointed in this museum. You taught me that I probably just don't understand this type of artwork."

Thad was quick with another quote, "Emerson also wrote, 'To be great is to be misunderstood."

"That's nuts!" I replied. "He wrote that, too? I'm going to have to buy a book by him. I'm happy I met you. I think I learned a lot from our conversation."

"If you learned anything from me during this conversation, just know that every work of art ever created is inexplicably authentic, whether you understand it or not," Thad said, as he looked at his watch. "Nice meeting you. I have to catch the train."

"Sounds good, Thad. You better hurry!"

"Naa... man, I don't like to hurry," Thad said. "Life is too long anyway."

After leaving the art museum in downtown San Francisco, I took a cab to a truck stop on Interstate 580. From there, I started hitchhiking to a small town called Tracy, about forty miles west. Luckily, I found another truck driver heading south on Interstate 5. It was around four in the morning when I finally arrived in southern California and called a cab to take me to Venice Beach.

When I reached the beach, I walked over to the ocean. It was beautiful out there. The moon cast a shimmering light across the ocean, and white-crested waves crashed onto the shore. I was thrilled to be there, so I removed my shoes and started walking where the Pacific Ocean met the California coast.

I fell asleep on the beach that night, not knowing it was illegal. There was some unique irony in this law because it was legal for homeless people to sleep pretty much anywhere else they wanted in California. In any case, I woke up the following morning to the sound of a beach patrol officer riding toward me with a modified dune buggy. The officer stopped his vehicle only a couple of yards away from my feet before he finally decided to turn off the vehicle. I tried to act like I was enjoying the scenery, but the officer knew better.

"Good morning," the officer said. "What are you up to, young man?"

"Actually, officer, I just got to southern California a few hours ago. I came to the beach to watch the sunrise over the ocean, and I must have fallen asleep." This would have been a good excuse, except it was pretty cloudy this morning, and the sun didn't rise over the Pacific Ocean.

"If you were expecting to see the sunrise on the western horizon, then you must be pretty disappointed in this morning's results, huh?" the officer responded with a goofy grin as he looked up into the sky and then back at me.

"No sir, I learned a lot about the ocean already this morning," I responded.

"I am sure you did, but whether you learned a lot or not, sleeping overnight on the beach is still illegal."

"Well, sir, I didn't know that," I answered. "And like I said, I wasn't intending to fall asleep. It was just an accident, really."

"How old are you?" the officer asked, as he took a tablet from his pocket.

"I'm eighteen years old. I just graduated from high school last spring."

"And what is your name, my man?"

"My name is Oliver."

"Okay, Oliver, can you wait here for a minute?"

At this point, it appeared to me that I was about to get into a lot of trouble when this officer called another officer and had a long chat about how to handle someone sleeping on the beach. After about five minutes of waiting around, I got asked more questions, like where I was from, where I was going, and what I was doing in Venice Beach.

I answered his questions as truthfully as I possibly could, leaving out that part of the reason why I was here was to seek revenge on the person who exploited my girlfriend. I also left out the fact that I was looking for my friend so he could help me harvest and sell a thousand marijuana plants. Then, just before I thought he was going to throw cuffs on me, he told me that I was free to go. I made it through that whole ordeal without anything stupid happening to me. I didn't even get a ticket. What a strange way to start a day.

I wandered around Venice Beach briefly before anything was even open. This gave me time to think about what I wanted to accomplish that day. With any luck, I would be surfing by noon, drinking beer by evening, and crashing at a cheap motel at night's end. I wrongly assumed earlier in the summer that surfing would be easy, considering I could skateboard pretty well. However, surfing was significantly more difficult than I expected. It took a while to get used to the waves and the ocean. I watched other surfers, and they made it look so easy, but I had very little luck. I tried for three hours straight, and I managed to catch only three proper waves.

Chapter XIV

I CALLED FREDRICK MULTIPLE times over the next few days. I also called Erica to inform her about my plans and let her know I had arrived in southern California. After much consideration, I decided to call my parents. However, when I called, my mom answered the phone and informed me that my dad had been arrested and was spending thirty days in jail, so he wouldn't be available to talk. Surprisingly, she didn't seem as upset as I had expected. She asked when I planned to come home. I lied and told her I found a warehouse job, so I wasn't sure exactly, but I mentioned that it would likely be soon. It was obvious that my mother was concerned about me. The conversation eventually ended with a heartfelt goodbyes and uncertain promises.

On the third day, I met one of the many girls with a perfect tan and wearing a string bikini as she was walking by me on the beach. Her name was Anika. After a brief introduction, she surprised the hell out of me by asking if I wanted to walk down the beach with her. At some point, Anika pulled out a joint to smoke and told me that she sold weed, which quickly created a bond of peculiar friendship between us.

Walking further down the beach, we talked about Anika's ancestry. I noticed she had a thick, French-Canadian accent, but she appeared to be Mexican. This combination was unusual enough that I felt comfortable asking her about it. "I'm 100% Mexican," Anika stated, "If my family were any more Mexican, we would all be playing in a mariachi band."

"Why don't you have a Mexican accent?" I asked.

"I was born in Canada," she said. "That is why I talk so slowly. I have to interpret three different languages before I understand what I am going to say."

"That doesn't make sense because Canadians speak English," I said.

"Not all Canadians... some speak French like me," she answered.

"But I thought you were Mexican?"

"I am," she replied. "I also speak fluent Spanish."

"Wow, I did not know this," I said. I thought Canadians spoke English."

"You thought wrong," I was born in Montreal, and pretty much everyone there speaks French and English. I guess it just depends on the conversation."

"What are you doing in southern California?" I asked. "Why aren't you in Canada or Mexico?"

"Have you ever been to Canada?" she asked.

"No, I guess I haven't."

"Have you ever been to Mexico?"

"No, I haven't been there either," I answered.

"Mexicans and Canadians are nice compared to people in America and exceptionally nice when compared to all the assholes here in Los Angeles."

"Why does this matter?" I asked.

"I hate everyone! That's why," she said. "Except for you, I like you for some reason. See, the last thing I want is to have some guy I don't even know selling some crazy Canadian pharmies or Mexican love potions to my friends. Who knows? They may get all whacked out and think that it would be funny to slip it into my beer when I'm not looking. Then, I would be out here on the beach trying to upscale my foreign competitors loving everybody rather than hating everybody, and that would suck! Wouldn't you agree?"

"You are kidding, right?" I asked, underscoring everything she just told me. I seemed to relate with Anika very quickly for a few different reasons. Although I didn't necessarily hate everyone, as Anika confessed, I could sympathize very easily when I compared it to my childhood and adolescence, when I'd get beat up and picked on.

"Kidding about what?" Anika asked.

"Nothing... go on..."

"It's about laws," she said. "I think politicians need to agree on something that makes sense! My plan would be like a giant nation-wide intervention. Every American would have to get involved in a gigantic act of patriotism and somehow pass a law that makes drugs less accessible. This law would increase the sentence for illegally manufacturing drugs in the United States by five hundred percent, which would scare the living shit out of those idiots cooking meth in their kitchen and whacked-out mother fuckers making PCP in their toilet bowl. One neglects to realize just how much of the nation's crime is committed by people high on drugs, possessing drugs, wanting drugs, and using drugs. With fewer drugs around, I think that most of these crimes would go away."

"What about weed?" I asked her. "What happens to all of the pot smokers?"

"That is simple... give every American the right to grow up to ten marijuana plants per household. Our government could even regulate this by registering individuals as certified marijuana growers. This law might even put some money in the pockets of people inclined to grow pot. This would not only increase the quality of bud, but it would stop drug cartels from shipping brick weed to the United States."

"Unfortunately, the government can figure out a way to fuck up anything," I said. "If it's not brick weed and cocaine, then it's going to be something else that ruins America. Probably, a drug that hasn't even been invented yet."

"Exactly," Anika responded. "The nation's war on crime is a scandal, and this injustice stands right in front of us all. Unfortunately, I had to learn this lesson the hard way while given the opportunity to do a different drug every day of the week since my first year in high school. Because of this, I fell victim to the life of a commodity drug dealer at a very young age. The sad thing is that I didn't know any better. The government provided me with drugs to sell, gave me the opportunity to sell them, and printed the bills in my pocket.

Our law enforcement is protecting a republic that likes to stand around with their heads up their ass. If a person was truly in the wrong place at the wrong time or just plain stupid, the charges should be dropped, and the entire nation should take responsibility for the crime. If justice were served, homeboy would get out of jail free, tell his friends and family why, and soon we would have a bunch of stupid people suing the government for the collateral damage it caused to their reputation. Once the government started to get kicked in the ass by the collaborative force of ignorance organized by the drug dealers of America, they would probably consider coming up with a solution to the nation's drug problem rather than just cashing in on their crimes."

Anika's obscure intellect and drawn-out theory of new American drug policies eventually led to a conversation about what had happened in my hometown. She was blown away by my story, especially the part about the buried money and marijuana field. She was so intrigued that she eventually asked me to return to her apartment for dinner.

I was excited to make a new friend, and everything was going great until her roommate came home. I was sitting at the kitchen table, and Anika was cooking dinner while still wearing a string bikini covered only by a tank top. There was no question that Anika was sexy as hell, but I wasn't there for that reason. Unfortunately, this was less than obvious to her roommate, who tried her best to make me feel unwelcome.

"Who the hell is this?" the roommate asked.

"This is Oliver," Anika responded, "and this is Jessica."

"It's great that you made a new friend, but it would have been nice if you had called me to let me know that we were having company over for dinner." Jessica stated just before she turned toward me with a look of contempt and said, "Before you get any ideas, I just want you to know that Anika and I are lesbian lovers, so you are not welcome here if you are anticipating having sex with Anika."

"Hey, Oliver never came on to me," Anika explained. "I invited him over for dinner because we had a great conversation. I didn't think it would be that big of a deal."

"Whatever," Jessica said, as she walked away, slamming the bedroom door behind her.

"I'm sorry, Oliver. I didn't know that she would get so pissed off. She must have had a bad day or something," Anika said. "Jessica has it in her mind that there is no room for men in this world, so she can be a bit of a bitch at times when she is around them. Especially if she thinks I have a sexual connection with them. See, I like to fuck men occasionally, and she likely thinks you are this man."

"Why are you with her if she constantly gets jealous?" I asked.

"Lots of reasons," Anika replied. "She's smart. She's funny, and she made me orgasm eight times last night."

"I'm glad that you found someone that makes you happy," I replied.

"Me too," Anika said. "Let me go talk to her to see if I can straighten this out."

During the next fifteen minutes, I overheard an intense fight in their bedroom. There was a long moment of silence and what seemed to be some reconciliation. Anika and Jessica eventually came out of their bedroom and apologized to me. A short while later, we sat down for dinner and discussed possible plans to harvest the weed in Nebraska. By the night's end, I agreed to give them three hundred dollars in rent money to crash on their couch for the next week or two while these plans came together.

Jessica and Anika were somewhat discrete about their lovemaking the first few nights as they wore robes around me and attempted to muffle their lovemaking. However, the wheels came flying off their bizarre attempt at discretion on the fourth night when Jessica decided to stop wearing clothes. She was over six feet tall and built like a brick shithouse. Her legs were like tree trunks, her ass would fill every bit of the biggest La-Z-Boy recliner she sat in, and she had the biggest tits I had ever seen. Meanwhile, Anika continued to wear clothes for the most part, which was a disappointment all the way around.

One night, we were all sitting around with the lights dimmed, watching <u>The Fugitive</u> with Harrison Ford. We ordered pizza, and everything seemed normal at the beginning of the night. However, about twenty minutes after the last piece of pizza was eaten, I looked over to the loveseat and saw Jessica and Anika fully engaged in lesbian sex. I'd nothing against lesbian sex, but this was low-key scissoring. This was some weird shit. I tried not to look at this abomination, but it wasn't easy, especially when Jessica started looking through the cabinets till she found a giant bottle of KY jelly. Looking over at me, she said, "Anika and I are about to do some really kinky shit, and we have decided that we want you to watch."

"I don't think I want to get involved," I answered, just as Anika came out from the bedroom holding a massive double-headed dildo and what appeared to be the world's largest butt plug. There were times when I would be intrigued by Anika and Jessica's lesbian lovemaking, but it was not one of those times. I was terrified! I started running around the apartment, tripping and falling all over the place. I was trying to find my backpack and shoes so I could get the hell out of there. Meanwhile, Jessica was bent over in the middle of the living room as Anika began to squirt a ridiculous amount of KY Jelly into her hand, ready for application. I didn't know what was about to happen, and I didn't want to know. As I was running out the door, I heard a loud, low-pitched moan coming from Jessica just before she yelled, "FUCK YEAH! It was as if she had just scored the game-winning touchdown at the Super Bowl.

About the time that Jessica and Anika scared the living shit out of me with their unique sexual prowess, I began to communicate with my nemesis nearly every day and soon realized that he had made a career out of being evil on a level way past what you'd see on Forensic Files or the Bad Boys TV series. This person seemed to be involved with every felonious crime known to man, including a weekend hobby of exploiting children.

Unfortunately, my nemesis didn't accept legal tender as a form of payment to acquire and remove Erica's naked body from the dark web, which made this painstaking situation substantially harder to resolve. However, after almost a month of bargaining, I finally felt that this goal would be accomplished when I agreed to commit a crime to advance his position in the criminal underworld.

The contracts that were initially discussed gave me all sorts of options to choose from. Unfortunately, all of these crimes were incredibly dangerous. They each posed a threat of getting caught by police or, worse yet, being murdered. Nevertheless, there were some upside advantages to completing one of these contracts, including compensation of at least thirty thousand dollars and exclusive rights to Erica's dark web exploitation. This would allow me to remove her naked pictures and videos from the internet permanently.

After a lot of thought, I eventually agreed to complete one of the more lucrative contracts with a criminal cartel known as T6. This assignment started in the early morning of September 3rd, 2001, when I took a bus to downtown San Diego and boarded the metro train heading south to Tijuana. I remember walking into Mexico through a weird-looking corral next to the highway and crossing over a shitty bridge where a bunch of kids tried to sell me pieces of gum called Chiclets.

The details of this contract were for me to meet a man at a bar called Mous Tache at noon, which was just a few blocks south of this bridge. Then, he would lead me into a bunker under the city where I would pick up a giant backpack filled with over two hundred thousand pills of Mexican pharmaceuticals to bring back to my nemesis. These pills consisted of Benzodiazepine, Morphine Adderall, and Steroids.

I arrived in Tijuana two hours early, allowing me time to visit a few street vendors selling Aztec calendars, beaded necklaces, and tequila shots. I remember these vendors tipping my head back and pouring the shot into my mouth while blowing a whistle. I'm certain that it will not make a difference how much time passes by, I will likely always remember the obnoxious tune played from these whistles.

The tequila helped calm my nerves when I went to look for the T6 cartel member with the backpack full of Mexican pharmaceuticals. The bar where we met was dark and dingy despite having no front wall facing the street. I remember this man being very short and having a wicked Mexican-styled mustache. He immediately showed me the gun he had tucked into his pants and told me that there were T6 Cartel members who would follow me until my contract was completed.

After this unsettling introduction, we walked across the street to a restaurant. This restaurant had a basement and a door that led to a thirty-foot tunnel. This tunnel brought us to a bunker filled with all sorts of firearms, drugs, and liquor. After a very brief conversation, I was given the backpack full of pharmaceuticals and the address in San Diego where I needed to deliver it.

At this point, I walked back through the city and once again stopped at some of these street vendors. I picked up two big, colorful Aztec calendars to give to my folks and Erica. Then, I took a few more tequila shots and crossed the border back into the United States. After catching the metro train headed north to California, I finally arrived at a Denny's restaurant in downtown San Diego at 4 pm. This is where I met another T6 cartel member, who exchanged the backpack full of drugs for an envelope containing thirty thousand dollars and a thumb drive with information regarding Erica's exploitation.

Then, I caught a bus in downtown San Diego and returned to Venice Beach. Once I arrived at my hotel room, I immediately plugged the thumb drive into my computer and followed the instructions to remove Erica's naked pictures and videos from the dark web. After a long, tedious process, I burst into tears when I finally accomplished my goal to remove this smut from the internet. At least this part of my nightmare was over.

Once my contract with the T6 cartel was completed, I started to get worried about my plans all falling apart on account of not knowing how to harvest or sell an estimated six hundred pounds of marijuana. I needed Fredrick to help me accomplish this goal. Unfortunately, I tried to call him every day since I arrived in southern

California, but he never answered. I began to think that I'd never see him again.

Just I planned to abandon my plans and return to Nebraska, I visited Fredrick's house one last time. I couldn't believe my eyes when I found Fredrick smoking a joint on his front porch. After so many days of nothing going right, I stumbled upon this glorious day when my life seemed to turn around. Seeing my friend made me incredibly happy.

"Holy shit!" I yelled. "It is actually you!"

"Oliver, my man, what the hell are you doing here?" Fredrick asked. "I thought you went back to Nebraska to marry your girlfriend or something like that."

"Well, I'm back," I said. "Where the hell have you been? I have been calling you every day for the last month."

"Sorry, I was on the East Coast tour with Phish," Fredrick replied. "I've been tripping balls on microdots for the last month. That acid is unreal! I saw your calls but was in the zone, Buddy."

"Look, man, I need your help!"

"What's going on, Buddy?" Fredrick asked. "How can I help?"

"I have a ton of weed back in Nebraska that needs to be harvested. Is there any way that you can help me out with this?"

"Maybe," he answered. "That would depend on a few things."

"Like what?" I asked.

"How good is the weed?"

"I'm nearly positive that it is primo."

"How much weed are we talking about here, Buddy? I ain't going out to Nebraska for less than a hundred pounds," Fredrick said. "By the time everyone gets their cut, there just isn't much left if it's less than a hundo."

"That's not a problem," I said. "I'm estimating up to six hundred pounds."

"Six hundred pounds?" Fredrick yelled. "You're going to need a semi-truck to transport all that."

"That was something I was going to ask you about," I replied, "How many lawns and leave trash bags are six hundred pounds of weed?"

"That depends on whether you plan to process it out there in Nebraska or back here in California," he replied.

"What do you mean... process?" I asked.

"You can't just cut down the plants and roll them into joints," Fredrick explained. "You need to clip the buds off the plants, and then you need to trim the leaves off of the buds. You also need to dry and cure it. It's a process."

"Shit, I never even thought of this. I was still trying to figure out how many people it was going to take to cut the weed down."

"That's the easy part," Fredrick said, "The trimming is what takes forever."

"Let's say I can find a place to process this weed in Nebraska. How many lawn and leave bags are six hundred pounds?"

"Between fifteen and twenty-five, thirty at the most," he answered. I guess it depends on how compact the bud is."

"What happens if I can't find a place to process the weed?" I asked. "How many lawns and leave bags will I need then?"

"Over a hundred bags, Buddy."

"I guess this means that we have to find a way to process it in Nebraska."

"Not unless you plan to load it all into a semi-truck and haul it all to Humboldt County," Fredrick replied, "I could probably get it all processed out there."

"Okay, so how much money are we talking about per pound?"

"I can probably charge up to fifteen hundred dollars a pound for processed bud, and maybe three hundred for unprocessed. I guess it depends on how good it is."

"Will you be able to move this much weed?" I asked, wondering how it would even be possible.

"Fuck yeah, I can!" Fredrick replied. "I can make weed disappear so fast it would make your head spin if it's primo like you say it is."

"Wonderful!" I said. "If this all works out, you will help save someone's life! My girlfriend's father needs a heart transplant, and they don't know how to pay for it. I have one more question."

"What's that, Buddy?

"Do you have any friends that can help with the harvest and processing?"

"I can call my pals up in Humboldt and see where they are at with things," Fredrick replied. "I'm pretty sure I can figure out something."

"You are the man, Fredrick! I'm so glad I finally found you!" I said, giving him a hug. "I'll swing by tomorrow after I talk to my girlfriend about the good news."

"That sounds like a plan," Fredrick replied. "See ya later, Buddy."

Chapter XV

After talking with Fredrick, I started to think through several challenges that I faced. The first was to ensure the weed was still growing on Billy's farm back in Nebraska. So, I called Erica and asked her to check on the marijuana field. Later that afternoon, she called me back, confirming that the field was untouched and ready to be harvested. I thought Billy's house, barn, and Erica's old house would be good places to process the weed.

The next issue was assembling a team to harvest and process this weed. Thankfully, Fredrick called some friends who were available for hire in Humboldt County. Anika and Jessica, as well as a couple of their friends, also agreed to help. Assuming Erica would pitch in, I was able to get fourteen people to commit to this harvest.

Now, I needed to arrange transportation. Not only did I need to figure out how to transport everyone from California to Nebraska and back, but I also needed to transport the harvested weed and two hundred firearms I planned to sell to the T6 cartel. Fredrick figured he could fit eight people in his van, and four people could fit in Anika's car. This meant that I still needed to arrange transportation for two more people in addition to the weed and firearms.

To solve this dilemma, I searched Craigslist for a large vehicle to purchase. After a few days, I found an old 1986 long-bed Ford

F-250 pickup truck. However, I still thought that this vehicle would be unable to transport everything back to southern California, so I found a 1981 box van that needed a little work. At this point, transportation seemed to be worked out. There would be fourteen of us going out to Nebraska in a hippy caravan consisting of Anika's almost brand-new 1999 Ford Taurus, Fredrick's van, an F-250 long-bed pickup truck, and a box van.

I convinced Anika to be the owner of the two vehicles I purchased on Craigslist and to get all the proper tags for an upfront fee of five grand. I also had to pay Anika's two friends for driving the trucks to Nebraska. I didn't plan out who would drive the vehicles back to California with all the weed and firearms, but I figured I would be one of these people. I knew that this would undoubtedly be extremely dangerous and could maybe result in me getting caught. However, my immature eighteen-year-old mind somehow justified the risk by calculating the reward for all of this.

At this point, I just needed to wait for the hippy to arrive from Humboldt County, and we were ready to drive to Nebraska. The plan was to assemble the crew on September 11th and then leave the following day. For the sake of brainstorming, I stayed with Fredrick for a few nights. After convincing Anika not to stuff giant butt plugs into Jessica's ass when I was around, I stayed a few nights with them as well.

The hippies arrived on September 10th, and everything was planned out and ready to go. Then, on the morning of September 11th, I remember waking up to Anika yelling, "Oliver, wake up! Check this out!" This was the morning of the 9/11 terrorist attacks in New York. For the next several hours, Anika, Jessica, and I watched the breaking news about the airplanes crashing into the Twin Towers. We didn't quite understand the gravity of this situation, so we joked about it and smiled about it. However, there was nothing funny about this at all. Three thousand people died in the attacks, and Dick Cheney was preparing to kill several thousand more for the sake of oil. The world seemed to stop for a couple of days following the terrorist attacks, so I decided to postpone our trip to Nebraska for a few days.

I was sitting at a bar in Venice Beach on September 13th. If everything went according to plan, our crazy hippy caravan would leave for Nebraska the following morning. This was a pretty eerie time in the nation's history. Everyone had a subtle look of fear on their faces. I can't remember if I felt an actual feeling of fear or not, at least regarding the terrorist attacks. I had far greater fears to be concerned with, and having a drink with a big, greasy burger seemed the best way to deal with them.

Some TVs hung above the bar, which were turned to the news about the 9/11 terrorist attacks. I had no invested interest in paying attention to this, but I still found myself staring at the TV simply because there really wasn't much else to look at. The restaurant was not very crowded, but nearly every seat at the bar was filled. However, there was plenty of shoulder room, so it felt like I had plenty of personal space. I had no plans to talk to anyone that evening, and I really just wanted to eat in peace and casually ponder my next move.

Everything was going fine until I heard the man beside me grumbling in my ear about his strong opinions regarding the terrorist attacks. At one point, he pounded his fist on the bar and turned to me to ask, "Can you believe this?" I let a moment or two pass, hoping this wasn't an invitation to share my opinion about the news.

Nevertheless, this man looked at me intending to start a conversation, so I vaguely answered his question by simply saying, "No." This is when he started to ramble about his political opinions. I felt strangely obligated to listen to him, or at least pretend to listen to him, simply because he would look a bit crazy sitting there talking to no one. I had no invested interest in this man's life, but I didn't want to be rude either.

"I hope Democrats clean house and gain control of Congress in the next election cycle," the man passionately stated before turning to me again to ask about my opinion regarding the matters of 9/11. "Can you believe how the United States is handling these fucking terrorist attacks?"

"Umm... I don't have any strong opinion about foreign affairs," I replied.

"You should," the man said. "This could lead to another pointless war! America always has to step in and save the day. I wish we had a sensible president who invested in the political concerns of inner cities and stopped sending money overseas. We are in the middle of a historical drug problem, homeless rates are near an all-time high, and don't get me started on the minimum wage. Nobody can survive on the minimum wage in this country. I can barely pay my rent, which is double the minimum wage. Absolutely no one can find a decent job in this city unless you are a dirty politician!"

"Yeah, fuck politicians," I said, hoping this would be the end of my interaction with this man. However, this was not where our conversation ended.

"You said it!" he responded. "If all the Republican crooks in this country were to die tomorrow, I would be ecstatic. Democrats like you and I need to vote these assholes out of office!"

When he said this to me, I suddenly realized a reflective thought, which was that I didn't know if I was a Republican or Democrat. Living my life in rural Nebraska and being raised as a Catholic suggested that my viewpoints were likely conservative, but I denounced my religion the moment I turned eighteen and hated how a small portion of the conservatives in Nebraska openly expressed their prejudiced viewpoints. I passionately rejected racism, homophobia, and every other form of social prejudice I had ever encountered.

I had a very vague understanding of politics and never invested any interest in learning about how the government worked. My government class in high school was right after the lunch break, so I was always baked. I also had no interest in learning about politics at this point in my life. Nevertheless, I now wanted to know what my political affiliation was. Not thinking through my approach to this at all, I turned to this man and asked a question that I would immediately regret, "What's a Democrat?"

When I said this, this man at the bar stared at me with an overly concerned and puzzled look. My face turned red as a long, awkward silence made me feel embarrassed and ignorant. Eventually, this uncanny moment of silence ended with the man at the bar asking me one of the most fundamental questions a United States citizen could ask, "You don't know what a Democrat is?"

To redeem myself from the obliviousness of government affairs, I stumbled over my best attempt at providing an intelligent response, "I know what a Democrat is... everyone knows what a Democrat is," I replied. "What I meant to say was... what does being a Democrat mean to you?" I really didn't have a clear understanding of what a Democrat was, but I didn't feel quite as stupid as I did a few seconds earlier.

"Holy shit!" The man at the bar remarked. "You had me worried for a second. There is nothing worse than being politically ignorant. I am a Democrat because I hate Republicans and their stupid ideas about how to run this country. They have never invested in the common welfare of anyone but business owners, who are all rich conservative assholes!"

I interrupted him as he said this because my family owned two businesses, and several people in my hometown owned a business. After giving this a quick thought, I realized that my family wasn't rich, and I couldn't think of anyone else who was particularly rich as a result of having their own business, either. Granted, where I had lived was a simple place, but I thought back to the conversation I had with Thad at the art museum in San Francisco, which made me realize that I was likely listening to a jaded viewpoint of someone who was at least a little ignorant himself. My response to this was instinctual when I said, "Not all business owners are rich."

"Okay, maybe not all business owners are rich, but the vast majority of them are, and they all vote Republican!" the man at the bar responded. "Capitalism is the root of all evil! I would love to see a socialist president get elected during the next election. Europeans get months of vacation each year and have a socialized welfare system. We have nothing in America but a bunch of gun-wielding nut jobs with a warped sense of freedom."

"Excuse my limited knowledge of foreign government. I never paid much attention in school, but how can Europe afford to pay for this?" I asked.

"Because their politicians actually care about people and are not all self-absorbed by their own agenda. European countries use their taxes to help the common welfare of their country and don't send billions of dollars to every goddamned country in the world that gets involved with any sort of military issue. We spend so much goddamned money on fighting pointless wars it is ridiculous. There hasn't been a single war that has made any sense since World War II. I could go on and on about how stupid our country is for not being more like Europe."

"The United States is much larger than any European country, so I'm sure achieving a socialized welfare system is harder. Our country also has the largest economy in the world. My knowledge of economics is also limited, but I can't imagine the world's largest economy was created by a fluke in capitalism. I understand what you are saying and think everyone should have free medical care. Having a lot more time off would also be a big advantage of socialism, but I think things are just different here, and we would be better off trying to figure out how to make our system of government better rather than trying to change it into something completely different."

"I disagree completely," the man at the bar interrupted. "We need a socialist revolution that defunds the military, taxes the rich, and subsidizes a better welfare system. Fuck capitalism and all the rich conservative assholes that run this country!"

"I understand some of your viewpoints and why socialism sounds more appealing than capitalism, but I don't think you can just change a three-hundred-year-old system of government that easily. Even if America one day voted for a socialist president, he would not be able to change everyone's mind about how our country should be run. Let's say America experienced some sort of political epiphany and actually decided to become socialist. Who is to say a socialized system of government would work in our country?"

"It works everywhere else in the world, so I am pretty damn sure it would work in America," the man at the bar responded.

"Are you telling me that every other country in the world is socialist?" I asked, expressing doubt that even the majority of the world has a socialized system of government, "I know for a fact that China is communist."

"China is an exception, but I seriously doubt communism would be any worse than capitalism," the man replied.

"I doubt that," I said.

"Are you a goddamned Republican?" The man asked with a clear sense of irritation. "That's it, isn't it? I knew there was something not quite right about you the moment I sat down. All you probably care about is banning abortions, supporting racist cops, and your goddamned gun rights."

"I am not a Republican, and sure as hell am not a racist!" I replied, now expressing my frustrations with this conversation's direction. Being called a racist really pissed me off, considering my convictions and moral judgment were the exact opposite of someone whose opinions aligned with racism.

"Well, you sound like one to me!" the man replied. "You sure as hell are not a Democrat!"

"If being a Democrat means being a self-righteous prick who thinks their opinions about America are better than everyone else, then I guess I am probably not a Democrat either. You know what else... I don't want to talk to you anymore about politics or anything else for that matter." After I retorted to this man's verbal vomit and attitude, I decided to get up from the bar to leave.

I didn't want to talk to anyone in the first place, and this person was precisely the reason why. In an attempt to elevate just how shitty his judgmental disposition made me feel, I spontaneously acted on a sudden feeling of generosity. After quickly counting how many people were in this bar and grill, I felt confident that I had plenty of cash to cover everyone's bill, so I took a big wad of cash out from my backpack, which instantly got the bartender's attention.

"I want to pay for the meals and drinks along with a 25% tip for everyone sitting at this bar right now except for this guy right here," I said, pointing to the narrow-minded dipshit sitting beside me. "This guy can go fuck himself with his stupid reasons he considers himself a Democrat."

At this point, the bartender started ringing a loud bell that hung above the bar and yelled out, "Hey everyone, this guy just paid all your tabs. Let's show him some appreciation." This caused everyone in the bar to start cheering and clapping. Just before leaving the bar, I looked at the dumbfounded man that inspired my unique reason for being so openhanded and told him with proper conviction, "Not all rich people are conservative assholes, you liberal prick!"

I understood the irony of calling someone a liberal prick and how my reaction to this man's judgmental opinions kind of made me a prick myself. As a self-proclaimed nice person, it was typically out of character for me to mindfully project cruel behavior without feeling bad about it. Incidentally, his initial statement about how the 9/11 attacks would likely lead to war was riddled with irony and strangely accurate. I wouldn't even discredit the fact that unchecked capitalism was destroying our country in many ways.

I came into that bar not knowing if I was a Democrat or Republican and left reasonably confident that I didn't want to be associated with or be judged by either party. I really didn't know anything about communism, socialism, or even capitalism, and this interaction with the man at the bar didn't exactly inspire me to invest much time in learning more about economics or politics. However, it opened my eyes to the fact that I had much to learn if I ever planned on engaging in an intelligent conversation about government. I knew that I was extremely limited by my own ignorance when it came to politics, but this was because of a lack of education rather than my inability to empathize with other human beings.

I went to bed that night with a better understanding of myself and what it meant to be a good person. In addition to just being nice to people and not projecting my shortcomings onto others, I realized how important it was to have an open mind. I understood it would take time and a lot of work if I planned to judge people only by their character, but at least I understood this assignment. I also knew it would be impossible to sympathize or empathize with everyone's problems and life choices. This meant coming to terms with the fact that many disagreements are unavoidable and may never be sorted. Most of all, I understood that I would have to admit to being wrong about nearly everything at least once before I ever planned on being right about anything.

Chapter XVI

I woke up on Anika and Jessica's couch the following morning with a slight hangover. I didn't know what was causing a worse hangover, the booze I drank at the bar or the asshat I was sitting next to. Either way, I needed to shake it off because this was the day a month of planning was scheduled to all come together. The girls woke up at about the same time as me. After taking turns in the bathroom, showering, and brushing our teeth, we each found our way into the living room. Jessica turned on the TV in search of something good to watch to pass the time until everyone was ready to leave for Nebraska.

Unfortunately, this was almost impossible because every station appeared to become a news station with a little scrolling screen at the bottom. The coverage of the 9/11 attacks was endless. Anika eventually gave up on TV and made everyone breakfast. During this time, Jessica and I combined forces to roll an epic joint to smoke. As much as we didn't get along when we first met, we had now developed a pleasant friendship.

After the joint was smoked and breakfast was eaten, some serious efforts were made to assemble the crew of people headed to Nebraska to harvest and process the weed at Billy's farm. We decided that everyone was going to eventually meet over at Fredrick's house because he had four of his hippy friends from Humboldt County, California staying with him. The other four were in a hotel only a couple blocks away from where I had paid for them to stay.

Meanwhile, Anika called her two friends, who each caught a cab to her apartment within the hour. Once her friends arrived, we smoked another joint, and then we all drove over to Fredrick's house to meet everyone. It took the entire morning to assemble our motley crew, but eventually, we got all our shit together and were ready to leave.

Everyone understood that we needed to be traveling light. This was because of the lack of room for luggage on the way back from Nebraska. I had been traveling light anyway and still had only a backpack to bring along. Anika, Jessica, and her four friends all managed to fit their belongings into small suitcases or duffle bags, which I thought to be about perfect for placating the boundaries created within the description of events we had prepared for.

However, the luggage situation for Fredrick and his hippy friends was truly an anomaly, which baffled me in several different ways. I first noticed a rather extensive collection of tools they would use to harvest and process the weed. I was extremely grateful for the hippies' forethought regarding all of this. I would have been put into quite a bind once we all arrived in Nebraska because pretty much all of these tools were proprietary to harvesting and processing weed.

The most puzzling part of their luggage was that not a single one of them appeared to have brought any extra clothing. Only a few of them even carried a handbag. All nine wore hippy clothes that reminded me a lot of how Jasmine, the girl I met in Seattle, had dressed. Plenty of corduroy and fabric patches created the framework for their ensemble of clothing. This included patches of artwork such as mushrooms, rainbows, and pictures of our sun with a smile on its face. Finally, no hippy would be complete without a couple of patches of Grateful Dead bears and trademark skulls.

Fredrick broke this common characteristic shared amongst his hippy friends because he seemed to have a lot of luggage to bring with him on this crazy expedition to Nebraska. He had four extremely nice hardcover suitcases and two coolers full of beer. In one of these suitcases, he had his clothes, which was to be expected, and another was full of snacks for when the hippies got the munchies. One was for drug paraphernalia, such as bongs and steamrollers, and the last one was full of drugs the hippies planned to consume over the next several days.

Fredrick made me pay for all these drugs upfront as payment for assembling his crew, which was in addition to what I would be paying him and his friends to harvest the marijuana. This mysterious man never seemed serious about anything, but he was not willing to negotiate on the amount of drugs that he planned to bring with him. In addition to the other upfront costs, this completely wiped out nearly all the money I had, which was about thirty-five thousand dollars.

This suitcase had two pounds of unbelievably good marijuana, which I didn't understand, considering that we were on the way to harvest an estimated four to six hundred pounds. Nevertheless, Fredrick seemed convinced that nearly all of it would be smoked just on the way to Nebraska. He seemed to be worried that there might not even be enough weed to get that far. In addition to this, there were also two pounds of mushrooms, twenty sheets of acid, and one pound of cocaine.

When Fredrick asked me to give him $6400 for cocaine, I obviously had concerns. However, he insisted that this was not negotiable because the hippies each consumed roughly an eight ball of coke a day when it came time to trim the weed, which would make this about a fifteen-day supply. My other primary concern was that I didn't understand how people with such insatiable drug habits could get any work done. That's when he convinced me that his eight hippy friends, along with about thirty-two others, formed a collection of people known as the Psychedelic 40, who were known to be the best marijuana farmers in the world. Fredrick didn't elaborate on this too much, but he told me that I was incredibly fortunate that the timing worked out. He said that large grow operations from all over the globe try to hire marijuana farmers from the Psychedelic 40 with little luck, and that if he hadn't spent years on Phish Tours with the leader of this collective, I wouldn't have stood a chance at retaining their services.

After working out all the drug problems and transportation issues, the plan seemed to come together. Fredricks's van was full-sized, so it managed to seat himself and seven of the hippies comfortably. I planned to ride with Jessica and Anika in the back seat with the one remaining hippy. I made it a point to hand-pick the person with the best hygiene, who happened to be the one of three without dreadlocks. Although the hippies didn't smell like ass like the people on my bus ride from Seattle to San Francisco, some of them still had some serious body odor to contend with, and nearly all of them smelled as if they just took a bath in patchouli oil. The exception to this was a large man named Bob. When we all left for Nebraska, I didn't know much about Bob, but he was as close to your average person as anyone from the Psychedelic 40. It's hard to describe what made this person an anomaly, but once you learn more about the hippies, this will make more sense.

I thought of driving one of the two transport vehicles I purchased, but I was still feeling uneasy about my warrants out of Nebraska, so I paid Anika's two friends five hundred dollars apiece to drive these vehicles in our crazy hippy caravan. These two girls were both ridiculously small people. Neither one of them was much over five feet. This made them look a bit odd as they were driving a big, older model box truck and a 1986 long-bed Ford F-250 pickup truck down the expressway, but this was far from the strangest thing about the hippy caravan.

What I would experience on the way to Nebraska would be an eye-opening experience for Fredrick and myself. This was an incredible group of people, but the world they lived in was profoundly different than the world you and I live in, so their presence was a continuous learning curve. We left Venice Beach around noon on September 14th, 2001, and soon found ourselves on Interstate Highway 15, heading west to Nebraska. If all went according to plan, I'd be standing in a field of marijuana with Fredrick and Erica in roughly twenty hours.